Praise for

The River and Enoch O'Reilly

"[Murphy] writes well about the voodoo effect of music, and the way that songs and stories can invade our dreams ... His Southern Gothic style [is] a cross between Flannery O'Connor and Flann O'Brien."

— *Times Literary Supplement*

"Murphy can write like an angel. Well, like a bad angel — a clarification he'd probably prefer. His gaze is mischievous, and he delights in words and can nail things and people with incisive descriptions that can be startling or funny but are always lucid. He has a showman's zest for the flamboyant, the baroque, the subverted cliché and lyrical phrase ... And he has a gift that is much rarer in writers than it should be: a sense of rhythm, a feel for the way sentences follow each other to carry the reader with them. Murphy is also a musician, and it shows." — *Irish Times*

+++++++

Praise for

John the Revelator

"An absolutely wonderful book . . . So fresh and so contemporary, so original and so disturbing and brave."
— **Colm Tóibín**

"Fabulous. It's some of the best writing I've seen from a younger Irish writer in a while." — **Colum McCann**

"Everything about *John the Revelator* excited me — I couldn't wait to turn the page and keep on going. It was like reading for the first time." — **Roddy Doyle**

"An original, music-haunted first novel . . . [A] noteworthy debut from a writer who sticks with his stormy vision of the world."

— *Dallas Morning News*

"In the hallowed pantheon of Irish coming-of-age novels, Murphy's strongly written debut splits the difference between the sensitivity of *Portrait of the Artist* and the freakishness of *Butcher Boy*."

— *Publishers Weekly,* **starred review**

"Peter Murphy's darkly gorgeous debut . . . is an Irish coming-of-age novel. It's also a meditation on why we tell stories." — *Cleveland Plain Dealer*

"[A] jaw-dropping debut . . . Murphy works literary alchemy on every page . . . This jarring tale of sonic youth dares readers to put it down. A terrific, disquieting addition to the long tradition of Irish storytelling."

— *Kirkus Reviews,* **starred review**

"Murphy has given the new century its own reference point with his soul-stirring debut novel . . . [with] line after line of inspired and, yes, revelatory prose."

— *Seattle Times*

"Charming and accomplished." — *Buffalo News*

"[An] incredible debut novel . . . This work establishes Murphy as an author of tremendous imaginative and linguistic power who has mastered Flann O'Brien's supernatural whimsy, Beckett's grim irony, and McCabe's unsparing brutality. Essential reading."

— *Library Journal,* **starred review**

"Marked by tight prose, memorable characters, witty dialogue and Murphy's singular voice."

— *Paste*

"Murphy writes spare, arresting prose with the brio of Ireland's current literary star Anne Enright and he has the ear for dialogue of Roddy Doyle."

— *Daily Express* (UK)

"*John the Revelator* is filled with lyrical prose, dark humor, and a remarkable degree of humanity. This coming-of-age story is the most engaging and adventurous debut novel I have read all year."   — *Largehearted Boy*

"A brilliant book."   — **Neil Jordan**

"Filled with humour and energy, and a certain sense of mystery . . . Very funny and original."   — **John Boyne**

"The prose is a bag of fireworks, crackling with idiom and humour. Domestic, mythic, creepy, funny. Brilliant."   — **Nick Laird**

The River and Enoch O'Reilly

ALSO BY PETER MURPHY

John the Revelator

The River and Enoch O'Reilly

Peter Murphy

Mariner Books
Houghton Mifflin Harcourt
Boston   New York

www.hmhbooks.com

First published in the United Kingdom by
Faber and Faber Limited in 2013

Library of Congress Cataloging-in-Publication Data is available.
ISBN 978-0-547-90477-1

Printed in the United States of America
DOC 10 9 8 7 6 5 4 3 2

For Paula

"And now, Enoch, I invented all things I have told you about, all you have seen on earth, all things you have written in these books . . . I have put a chart on earth and ordered the ages to be preserved, and the writing of your fathers to be preserved that it will not perish in the flood I shall unleash upon your people."

— *The Book of the Secrets of Enoch*

Prologue

The Rua it was named because of its rusty colour when it gnashed and roared in flood, pouring through the valley's slopes to finally consummate with the sea at the mouth of Ballo Harbour.

On the first day of November in the year of '84, that enduring river turned on the town of Murn. You will remember it if you were there: clouds gathered overhead like great black cattle, the sun dimmed and the air was charged with augury, a sense of the imminent, the never-heard-tell-of close at hand.

The things of nature sensed it first. Rats could be seen ferrying their young further up the incline of the bank. Horses were skittish, dogs chewed their leashes. No birdsong could be heard – even the wizened, weird old herons had disappeared. Spiders climbed the branches of the trees to spin new webs, cocooning the leaves with silver gauze. And down the banks a boy gathering insects in a jar stared mesmerised as worms emerged winding from the soil.

The rain began. Spots of water smacked off the paths and then the downfall quickly thickened to a deluge that within an hour flooded the gutters and left the roads slick and gleaming. All day long rainfall flogged the grass and stones and beat down the sycamores and stripped the cones from the stands of pines. The current picked up speed and the river swelled to the lip of its banks and churned muck turned it claret. And now the siege was on.

The hard men and the horseshoe-throwing boys smoked and spat and kept watch on the river's rise from the doorway of the saddlery, making wagers on when the swell might gain the quay. Two more days of steady downpour it took, and then that renegade Rua breached its embankments and almost at once the promenade was a lake that rose and kept on rising until landmarks were submerged. One entire oak, old and rotten but still a mighty oak, was pulled from its moorings and upended completely, and then drifted off like a toppled god. There were landslides on the railway track, all services suspended. The handball alley filled with dirty sluicewater, rubbish floating on the surface like bits of shipwreck. Local radio issued flood damage updates on the hour. Everywhere was besieged and soaked as that bloated old river conquered the valley slopes and threatened the town's worried heart.

Nearly a week of this before the rain eased off and the sky began to clear. On the morning of November seventh, the first full day of pale sunlight following six long days of gloom, the body of Iggy Ellis, a twenty-six-year-old security guard with an address at New Larkin Park, was found washed up some three miles downstream. Some said he'd been seen in Hyland's the night before, throwing shorts down his neck as if to douse a fire.

Two days after that, the centre-forward for the under-twenty-one hurling team, Owen Cody, was recovered by a dredging crew clearing silt from the river's bed – some said he'd stormed out of a training session after a row with the trainer Tommy Lennon. That Sunday night, twenty-five-year-old single farmer Isaac Miller got up from the breakfast table, filled his pockets with stones, went for a walk and did not return. Then the remains of an unidentified male were found floating in a still pond under the railway bridge at the end of the promenade. And on November twelfth the body of fifth-year student Nicky Wickham was recovered at Marlhole Point.

The number of those drowned or reported

missing continued to rise as the flood ran its course. Townsfolk were called down to the morgue to identify bodies, some relieved when they couldn't verify the deceased, others when they could. Television and radio crews appeared and reporters thrust out microphones and questioned locals about this drowning epidemic. The locals clammed up or stammered if you please to be left alone.

By now the floodwaters had begun to draw back within the river's banks. Waterfront residents readied themselves for the dismantling of floodgates and sandbag dams as plumbers and electricians poked through debris. The riverfront was a jumble of furniture, ruined books, skips filled with sodden bits and pieces. Restoration of quayside properties would run to many thousands, the wireless said. But the world beyond Murn continued on: reports of nuclear power protests and the latest on the miners' strikes, fallout from the Brighton Hotel bombings, famine in Ethiopia, four more years of Ronald Reagan.

On the morning of Sunday November eighteenth, eighteen days after the rain began, the parish priest Father John Callaghan approached his pulpit in St Cecilia's church. His face that day was gaunt, and his eyes were clouded as they searched and beseeched the faces of the congregation. He spoke into the microphone and the church resounded with a single word.

'Why?'

They sat in rows, the survivors, the plodding on, heads bowed and hands clasped between their knees, both embarrassed by the priest and for him, because they had no answer to the question. The only one who knew was God, and no one would presume to speak for Him.

The priest invoked the Great Flood in the Bible and wondered if their earth so offended the sight of Our Lord that He would smite them with another deluge, and that the river would steal away so many. He voiced disbelief that the town of Murn could have affronted God so grievously that He would renege on His promise – rainbows our reminder – to never again destroy the world with water. Next time, He had promised, it would be with fire.

'Is our wickedness so great? Is mankind beyond redemption?' the priest demanded. 'I say that we are not. If we are to be saved, however, we must petition Him. We must raise our voices in prayer and let our virtue shine to the heavens, that He might see our goodness and spare us this affliction. The cursed folk of Egypt once marked their doors with blood so that the spirit of death might pass and spare their firstborn sons. We will not mark our doors with blood. We will confront darkness with light. We must put candles in the windows of our hearts, lit by the fire of the Holy Ghost.'

At this point he came down to stand among the congregation, and even now, without the benefit of amplification, his every syllable was heard.

'I do not know whether this flood is God's will or Satan's,' he said. 'My name is not Noah and this church is no ship all covered in pitch. But we can make it our ark. We can shelter here from the flood's wrath and take refuge in prayer and hymn and wait until the first bird returns with the leaf held in her beak.'

With this he swept back up the aisle and regained the pulpit and stooped so close over the microphone you could hear his every breath.

'Until that day,' he said, 'when a new rainbow lights up the sky, we must be vigilant. Because we know neither the day nor the hour, nor whom the river will next take.'

And now he turned away from the congregation. The front rows all sat with faces ashen, aware that many friends and relatives of those lost were present, still raw with grief. Even the bovine old boys at the back of the church smelling of pub and wet dog, their overcoats fuming as they leaned against the radiators – even these old duffers shuffled with discomfort.

The priest's words were answered by the river. That week she returned three more bodies. On Monday November nineteenth a man's remains were spotted snagged in weeds by the slipway, so old and decayed the medical examiner could not estimate a time of death – he might have been a decade in the water, maybe longer. Then a young woman's body was recovered at the mouth of Ballo Harbour on November twentieth. Then Billy Litt, yard man at Carbury's Abattoir, found November twenty-first.

And then it stopped.

Three days, five days, a week without further fatalities, and the town of Murn held its breath. Within ten days of the last reported disappearance, all but two of the bodies had been recovered. News reports took on an air of finality. Over a period of fourteen days, nine souls, most of them aged between eighteen and twenty-seven, were taken by the river. Some of the papers put the toll as high as twelve, some as low as eight, but they were mistaken.

No one had an explanation. No local wanted to discuss it. If mentioned at all, it was obliquely, furtively, because it resisted all logic. Officials talked of inquiries, sociologists spoke of in-depth studies, but when the death count halted and it became clear that there was nothing more to say, the television crews and reporters and professors packed up and moved on.

The end of November brought bitter winds that petrified the fields. The Rua froze solid for the first time in twenty-eight years, gleaming like a hockey rink under the sodium streetlights. Children sported and skated upon the river's banks, oblivious to the secrets sealed beneath. Folk stopped indoors and built fires and ran hairdryers over pipes and the talk was of water shortages and a near-religious longing for a thaw.

On the feast of St Francis Xavier, quayside residents and hotel guests were woken by gunshot reports and a local man was seen on the slipway, shotgun stock braced against his shoulder, discharging rounds into the Rua. But no matter how many shells he pumped into the ice, he could not kill the river. The squad car arrived and Sergeant Davin appealed to the man to put down the gun. The man fled, and the ice began to crack.

Slowly things returned to normal, or what passed for normal. Christmas was a painful affair for many households, but it came and went, and soon a new year had begun.

And so the deep wound the river carved began to heal in time as the events of that winter receded in the common memory. The nightmare faded, became assimilated into lore, an old fable or a fairytale curse, the details growing ever murkier. Only the river knew, and the river wasn't telling.

This is all years ago now, of course. The young probably know little of it while their elders prefer to let the matter lie. But it's never far from certain minds, certain souls who hear the river and remember that early winter, like a recurring dream of a time outside of time, a month on no calendar at all.

Sometimes the river's current sings soothingly in their dreams, babbling its lullaby. It says it knows where the bodies are buried, but will keep their secret, all their secrets, the whole town's secrets, the river air malarial with secrecy. Thou shalt not kill, the river whispers, is only the fifth commandment. Compared to certain ends, death is a mercy.

And in their dreams the townsfolk do not speak. Because they do not wish to rouse the river.

I

ENOCH O'REILLY AND THE HOLY GHOST RADIO

Enoch's Last Stand

31 October 1984, the night before the flood

Deep inside the bowels of Ballo Manor, Enoch O'Reilly sits in a swivel chair in his father's cellar, staring gloomily into the flickering screen before him.

His mind is churned to froth by the whirl of choppers' rotor blades, the *whomp-whomp-whomp* of herons' wings. A sine wave pattern eddies across the glass. His face is rendered Hallowe'enly by the light cast from that cold intelligence, an unblinking eye into which a man might look (and be looked upon, some say).

This man looks like death warmed up: wax complexion, hair lank and manky, his eyes sad pools beneath the black ice of tinted lenses. Yes, Enoch O'Reilly has borne and witnessed better days. See how his hand trembles as it tips Glenfiddich into a china teacup and then he knocks it back and broods and fumes and broods some more and thinks FINKS, SONSABITCHES and many other epithets for the demons that besiege his brain, hell-bent on his ruination as they ruined other giants of men before him.

Enoch gulps the last of the malt and hurls the teacup against the wall and the cackle that follows sounds a bit non-sequitur hanging in the air, a bit oops-upside-the-head. He pushes his swivel chair back on its wheels revealing the Anson & Deeley boxlock-action double-barrelled shotgun broken open across his knee. Two bright orange cartridges wide as Smarties tubes are snuggled in the breech, and suddenly he is very weary, weary in his bones and in his balls, no two ways about it, sickandfuckin-tired of life itself, twenty-seven years of this shit and in the end it comes to less than naught.

So this is Enoch's last stand. The siege is near its end, and here is where a man might discern the stuff of which he's really made. They will not lock him in a rubber room to rave away his days. Enoch O'Reilly will leave this world like a fucking warrior monk.

He removes his glasses, bought so many moons ago when Elvis Presley still walked up and down upon the earth, may God have mercy on his soul. The frames are large and ostentatious, almost aviat-or shades, tinted like a limo's windows. One thought begets the next and now it's the King besieged by his own demons and discharging firearms indoors and spouting Corinthians: *We see through a glass darkly, friends . . . When I was a child I spoke like a child but there comes a time we put those childish things away . . .*

But here we must interrupt our ruminations, for Enoch snaps the shotgun shut. His uncanny eyes stare into twin-barrelled nothingness and see his own nothingness reflected. He bends his head almost reverently and his lips engulf the cold metal of the barrel. His thumbs conspire around the triggers, and the metal tastes so very sour.

Now, as Enoch's thumbs curl tighter, an old joke jackintheboxes in his thoughts.

What's the last thing to go through a fly's mind when it hits the windscreen?

Its arse.

A cheap gag.

A cheaper one: go on breathing long enough and you become your father, hardwired to do the very things you swore you never ever would. Your parents might deny you the facts of life, but never the facts of death. They teach you by example and suddenly they disappear off the face of the earth or rot away in hospital wards tended by sad-eyed country nurses. Yes, our parents die and teach us how to die in turn.

He will not go like that.

So hold your breath, for now Enoch's thumbs, they whiten.

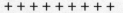

Enoch O'Reilly & the King

1956–1969

Enoch O'Reilly then. Born into a big old house known as Ballo Manor, twenty miles south of Murn, just beyond the village of Mweelrooney – although they won't thank you for reminding them – in December '56, the year that Elvis released 'Blue Moon'. And just as the King was Gladys's pride and joy (and what a name was Gladys Love Smith) Enoch too was his mother's dote. He was not the first seed to take root in her womb, but the first she brought to term, and grateful for an answer to her nightly petitions she spoiled her only child with meringues and tarts until he was round and plump. He has such lovely eyes, she said, his father's eyes, though the neighbours thought them almost goatish.

Throughout the tender years the boy longs to meet his hero Elvis Aaron Presley and torments himself with fantasies of what it would be like to sit and converse with the King. During study sessions at Christian Cub Camp – his mother's idea – when bogged down by the Bible's begats and endless miracling and parabling, Enoch finds that if he simply swaps the multifarious names of God with Elvis, the riddles of scripture reveal themselves and he can commit vast tracts to memory.

Presley's *40 Golden Greats* (Pickwick) provides Enoch's childhood soundtrack, a Christmas gift only surrendered by his mother Kathleen after she'd inscribed the sleeve with a quote from St John's gospel: '*Little children, keep yourselves from idols.*' Softly crooned spirituals and sentimental songs such as 'Peace in the Valley' and 'Old Shep' soothe Enoch's Sunday mornings, while on Saturday evenings boogie-woogie numbers like 'Hound Dog' and 'Jailhouse Rock' rumpus through that creaky, draughty parlour. His party piece those evenings is 'Heartbreak Hotel' with a hairbrush for a microphone, Kathleen beaming, his father barely hiding a pained grimace.

A former radio operator in the army, Frank O'Reilly has the appearance of a military man to the soles of his spit-shined shoes. Never once does Enoch see his father in pyjamas or dressing gown. The man is booted and suited within seconds of his clock's shrill alarm, always set for 5 a.m.

Frank for his part often expresses concern to Kathleen over his boy's soft hands, the folds of belly like flabby grins, and is forever sending Enoch out of that dank and mildewed house to get a lick of sun on his face or walk some of the blubber off, even though he himself spends every hour God sends in shadow.

A driven man is Frank O'Reilly, no sooner home from his electrical business in Mweelrooney than he disappears into his cellar to listen to meteorological reports and consult charts and sit with headphones clamped over his ears. His workshop is kept under strict lock and key. Enoch's curiosity about that forbidden room begins to grow.

One night when the household is asleep he steals downstairs. He removes the cellar key from the jamjar where Frank hides it and the torch from beneath the sink. Then he unlocks and opens the cellar trapdoor and stares down into the gloom. The air seems static there, charged with energy, and Enoch feels the hairs twitch on the back of his neck. He screws up his nerve to the sticking point and forces himself to go down those steps. Only when the hatch is closed behind him does he shine the torch around his father's workshop. The floor is strewn with radio equipment: shortwave units, crystal sets, Hertz transmitters, spark-gap receivers, Vibroplex bugs and Branly coherers all arrayed in various states of disassembly. On the walls are arcane shipping charts and maps with markings in old Irish or strangely spelled English.

Young Enoch shudders. It is cold. He swings the torch-beam towards the work bench and takes in the components and parts, transistor circuits abandoned mid-surgery, loose wires and batteries, valves and solenoids, magnetic tape reels, bits of Morse trans-mitter keys and two-way radio sets. Dominating the worktop are an aerial, monitor screen, keypad and microphone. Headphones hang from the handle of a vice, umbilicalled to the input by a cord. Under the bench squats some sort of printing press.

Enoch examines the machine's display. His fingers grope its backplate until they find a master switch, then flip it. The machine hums and buzzes and its display greenly glows. In the top right-hand corner, the date and time, his father's name, and a readout: ETF 5597 DAYS.

Sound leaks from the headphones. Enoch slips them over his ears, fearful that his parents might hear. Through his head shoot outer-space noises, whistles, bleeps and static. His hand hesitates over the dial – if he meddles with this machine, his father will surely know. But that pale and chubby hand twists the dial and the needle moves through the frequencies. Enoch hears what sound like babbling languages and his skin tingles and his scalp tightens on his skull.

Still that hand rotates the dial. Now music: saloon pianettes and autoharps, an old crone's warble. Another quarter twist, another song, but he can barely discern the words through the frying-pan static. Enoch twists the knob some more and now it's classical music, then someone recites a poem in a foreign language and then a blast of some language that's no language at all, and then a preacher's voice, no mistaking its fury:

'. . . *HOLY GHOST RADIO, transmitting for your benefit the sounds of the DEAD . . .*'

The voice sounds possessed. Enoch cannot move.

'*Now hear this, heathen men,*' it roars. '*There were giants on the earth in ancient days. The sons of God came unto the daughters of men, and they bore children to them, and the same became mighty men which were of old, men of renown. And God saw that the wickedness of man was great in the earth, and that every thought of his heart was only evil continually. And it repented the LORD that He had made man on the earth, and it grieved Him at His heart.*'

Those words, that voice: instant recognition. Something inside the boy sings out: I *know* this. His lips move, anticipating each syllable, as the preacher fumes and fulminates. He does not understand how he knows these words, but he knows them at his core. They are like great black wings beating in his ears.

'Then God said unto Noah, the end of all flesh is come before me, for the earth is filled with violence through them, and, behold, I will destroy them with the earth. And, behold, I, even I, do bring a flood of waters upon the earth, to destroy all flesh, wherein is the breath of life, from under heaven; and every thing that is in the earth shall die. And He loosed on men His fierce anger – all His fury, rage, and hostility. He killed the oldest son in each family, the flower of youth throughout the land. And He turned their rivers into blood.'

The voice becomes engulfed by static. Language lapses into a sort of glossolalia, the warping sounds of a tape being eaten up. Enoch wrenches the headphones from his head. Panic constricts his chest and lungs. He does not know how he anticipated those terrible words of flood and death and blood. Breathe, he commands himself. Breathe. Bile comes up his throat and he flees from the cellar, retching and groping blindly.

Enoch lies awake that night, hugging himself, struggling to make sense of what he's heard. The preacher's words have mortified him, but also charged him with dark electricity. He longs to see that preacher's face, to look into his eyes and know the mind of the man whose tongue can transmit such power. He feels at once damned and saved, fallen and raised up, and even when he falls asleep he shivers in his dreams, for Elvis Presley comes to him dressed in a long frock coat, a gilded bible in his hand. His perfect hair shines with unguent and his soft eyes gleam and he speaks with the voice of a man who thinks he is a god, or perhaps a god who thinks he is a man:

'See how one mortal soul can preach fear into the many. Now go forth Enoch. Go forth and find the source of the Holy Ghost Radio and steal the preacher's fire for your own. Do this and you shall have dominion over all kingdoms and principalities, and you shall never be beholden to any sonofabitch who walks up and down upon the earth's cold crust.'

Early the next morning Enoch wakes to see his father standing over his bed, fury in his eyes.

'You were meddling with my radio,' his father says. 'Nothing works any more.'

All Enoch can think to say is that he's sorry.

'Years of work,' Frank says. 'Do you understand? Your stupid fiddling has destroyed my work.'

Enoch risks a reply.

'It wasn't like other radios. I could tell what it was going to say.'

'Well it's not saying anything now, is it?'

Frank tugs at the cuffs of his shirt.

'Not a word about this to your mother.'

Enoch cannot face the drive to school that day, and when Kathleen calls him for his porridge, he feigns sickness. He does not breathe freely until he hears the front door slam and Frank's Ford Cortina drone away into silence. His mother fusses and clucks and feels his forehead and brings the wireless for company, but Enoch does not switch it on. All day he stays under the bedclothes, and when he finally ventures downstairs he sees the lock's been changed on the cellar door.

As that summer wears on Frank comes home later and later at night, sometimes not 'til dawn. His appearance begins to change. His hair grows long and he often goes unshaven and young Enoch begins to regard him as something beyond a man or a father, something almost supernatural.

One August morning he wakes from a stale semi-sleep, still damp from the residue of a dream or memory – he cannot decide – in which he and Frank were out walking the fields, trudging through briars, ducking under electric fences. His father's shotgun was broken over his arm and his eyes scanned the sky for crows. In a grove he stripped a branch from a hazel tree. 'The earth has bubbles,' he said, 'as the water does. And this –'

He held the branch aloft.

'– is the boy to find them.'

For days Enoch searches the dream or memory for meaning, but it yields nothing he can comprehend. Then, one bright and terrible morning in September of '69, his mother tells him the news. Frank has had an accident. It was quick and painless, Kathleen says. His father didn't suffer. He will be planted within days, but Enoch is to be denied the funeral and the viewing of the corpse. Too distressing, his mother says.

She will not meet her boy's uncanny eyes.

+ + + + + + + +

Enoch O'Reilly's Schooldays

1970–1974

Enoch O'Reilly hates his five years at St Ignatius's Juniorate in Murn. He hates the austere corridors hung with portraits of grim and joyless icons, po-faced cardinals and popes in skullcaps and purple robes. He hates the cabbagey, condensationed nights when there is nothing to do but stare at the ceiling and tug on your plum until sleep comes. More than anything he hates the other boarders, their uncouth ways, their farty smells and greasy fingers, their mickey-and-fanny jokes, the way they ridicule his weight.

They'll end up fodder for the ESB or Civil Service, he consoles himself. Their future is mapped in advance like dance steps at a dry Feis, birth-school-work-death, the only likely variation being which technical college they'll attend or which rugby club they'll spend the weekend at sinking Harp or Bass before returning to the Monday morning grind, slaving and saving with the Credit Union until such time as they wed some stalwart local lass, put their mark on the council house list and set about issuing a brood of bawling, cowslicked spawn to perpetuate their name.

But for now he is trapped among their number. He had imagined that his tenure in the Juniorate might help him understand that terrifying preacher's voice, those words of flood and death and blood. He assumed his classes here would enlighten him as to how such men scare hellfire into those who oppose the will of God – or at least the will of God as interpreted by those who operate in His name. Alas, it is a Christian Brothers school, where the young are deemed unfit to study scripture with their own eyes, and must receive the word of the Lord second-hand, chewed to baby pap by their teachers or in the Abridged Children's Version, minus the dirty, bloodthirsty, incesty bits.

But young Enoch decides he needs no intermediary to translate or bowdlerise the Word. He buries his face in the King James Bible, Genesis to Revelation, Numbers to Corinthians, Deuteronomy and Leviticus and the Epistles and the Gospels. For entertainment he devours the tale of crazy Ahab's quest to kill the whale that took his leg, and for moral instruction Shakespeare's escalating cycles of betrayal upon betrayal, revenge upon revenge, witches and ghosts, Titus's twisted lusts, Richard's hump, Hamlet's ghost, Banquo's ghost, rivers of blood, Duncan's blood, Banquo's blood, the blood of Macduff's wife and babes, the blood of Macbeth himself. These are his true teachers now, Enoch is their ward, and in time he decides that he does not believe in God. He believes in the power of the Word, the Word he heard that night in his father's workshop, a voice railing over those frequencies like Ahab across the waves.

Now come nights when he dives under the covers and sips altar wine stolen from the Juniorate's chapel vestry, and the last thing he sees before his eyes close is the framed photograph on the wall opposite his bed: Elvis, Jerry Lee Lewis, Johnny Cash and Carl Perkins gathered around a piano in Sun Studios on a December day in 1956. This is the fabled Million Dollar Quartet, the four horsemen of the rockabilly apocalypse whose ruckus resonated louder than the H-bomb through the post-war void when anything seemed possible because everyone was doomed, when mankind first possessed the capability to annihilate itself and so every threatened moment counted, because all they had was now, because tomorrow might never come, and this sense of existential peril bestowed upon their music the molten heat of madness: Elvis's jailhouse rock, Jerry Lee's great balls of fire, Johnny's ring of fire, Carl's St Vitus Dance.

What a thing it must be, thinks Enoch, to have such friends.

+ + + + + + + +

Every schoolyard has its scourge. The Juniorate's is Billy Litt, sixteen years of age, hatchet-faced, his fists afflicted with warts. The moment his and Enoch's eyes lock is like some black parody of sexual frisson: two souls recognise each other across the Darwinian line that partitions predator from easy meat, and Enoch wonders if there isn't something written in his physiognomy that begs for dog's abuse. Their first meeting becomes the stuff of legend. Here is an account.

Enoch is sat in the shelter of the Juniorate's exercise yard, head buried in a paperback about a former Mau Mau who gets stabbed and sees the light and becomes a slum missionary, when Billy strides across the yard and snatches the book from his hands and dangles it out of reach.

'Give that back or I'll kill ye,' Enoch says.

Billy stuffs the book under his armpit.

'You're dead, son,' he says. 'You're *claimed*.'

Billy's cronies gather around like hyenas and jeer their mark. *Lard-arse! Homo! Gowl!* and other ugly terms lodge in Enoch's mind, and he calls upon the Holy Ghost to inflict a pox upon their houses and make their balls rot off.

'Handball alley!' someone yells, and before you know it the thing takes on its own momentum and the handball alley it is, and they're swarming across the road and chanting *fight-fight-fight* down the gas-yard lane towards the hulking graffiti-covered wreck on the promenade. One at a time they duck through the door-shaped gap in the brickwork. The older lads sit on rotten girders that serve as seats and rekindle butts and swing their legs and wait for the action down in the court.

Enoch enters the centre circle. Billy Litt throws the paperback to the ground and rolls up the sleeves of his bomber. Enoch musters all his nerve and drops his head and charges for the book, but Billy matadors aside and grasps him in a headlock and lands swift digs in the face. Blood raspberry-ripples from Enoch's nose and down his chin, but he wrenches himself out of Billy's hold and back-pedals to get his wind back. There's no sound but their heavy breathing. Then, as Billy's about to make his move, there's a sort of wave effect of boys backing away from the alley's entrance. The spectators all stand for a better look.

Something pokes itself through the low opening and enters the court, all angles and points, the movements strangely clockwork. Its feathers are manky and tattered.

'You must be fucking joking,' Billy says.

The heron moves between the staring boys, who part and draw back as if from a thing deformed. Claws clack on the cement as it steps across the playing area, and its angular head moves as though on bearings. The beak is a harpoon's tip. Strange eyes dart from one lad to the next.

Barely is there time to absorb this when a second heron enters and stop-motions across the floor. All eyes are on these unearthly twins, but not a word is said. Then comes another. All told, three of these weird birds position themselves around the alley's perimeter, perfectly still like sentries, only their slitted, sideways-blinking eyes betraying any movement.

The moment is frozen. No sound except for the sibilant wind in the trees and from beyond the alley's high walls the soft music of the Rua. Enoch snatches up his book and darts between the sentry herons and out of the court and across the green. He scrambles over the rim of the bank and crouches out of sight at the water's edge among the reeds and bulrushes. Schoolboys stream out of the handball alley and stand in a bewildered silent pack, avoiding one another's eyes. Even Billy Litt is mute. The air is static and crackly and each boy suddenly wishes to be away from this place. The crowd disperses up the gasyard lane.

Enoch sticks his head above the lip of the river bank. No sign of the herons. No one on the prom. He places his book on the grass, and his chubby fingers pluck a dock leaf from its root and dip it in shallows rainbowed with pollutant, and he uses the leaf to daub his nose and mouth, like an artist cleaning his palette.

That night as Enoch kneels before his framed photograph of Elvis and pals he remembers the King's instruction and makes a solemn vow to never again be put upon by any sonofabitch who walks across this earth. In bed he feels vast muscles in contraction, forcing him towards his fate. The way ahead is clear. When he completes his Leaving Cert he will enter St Mark's Seminary and study for the priesthood. He will inherit that Holy Ghost fire, breathe it into his lungs, become luminous with its heat.

For those who cannot do – the Brothers and their laity – teach. But the priest, like the sorcerer before him, and the druid before him, *acts.* He seizes power and wields it. He walks through fire to forge the iron of his character. He tests his mettle against the furies and the fates. He knows the stuff of which he's wrought. He does not fuck about. The priest occupies the true seat of power, to which it's Enoch's destiny to ascend.

Once ordained, will he go on to minister in the missions? No, he will not. Will he carry out good and charitable works? By no means. A modicum of fame, then, a soupçon of power? All this and much more. Ambition does not always know its end, but its beginnings are palpably manifest in the guts of those who nurture it, and whom it nurtures. Here then is Enoch's vow: to preach like that voice on the Holy Ghost Radio, whether he believes in God or not. Enoch O'Reilly will not cease from manual labour nor mental fight until he has transcended the muck of his origins and stolen the preacher's thunder and become nothing less than incandescent.

+ + + + + + + +

Enoch O'Reilly in St Mark's

September 1975

His ordination suit and a knee-length frock coat, his soutane and surplice, his stole and breviary. A pair of shaded glasses bought at a flea market that summer. A chunky rosary hung between the buttons of his black silk shirt, unbuttoned to the breastbone.

This is Enoch O'Reilly's uniform, his armour, paid for with the cut of his father's pension that his mum sends on the first of every month, along with the odd postcard from Lourdes or Medjugorje. Kathleen has taken to touring the basilicas, funded by the payout after Frank's death. Enoch enrols in St Mark's seminary, twelve miles south of Murn, just beyond Ballo Harbour. The application form was the work of only moments, the evaluation process minimal. All that's left is an informal interview with the Dean, by all accounts a joyless specimen.

It is 1975 and the seminary is desperate for new blood. Ordinations are in decline. The board has decreed the curriculum be expanded beyond the ecumenical and ecclesiastical to include the arts, sciences and humanities. The telecommunications module is now among the best in the country. Enoch totes his belted suitcase across the cobbled quadrangle just as the secular shareholders are throwing the baby Jesus out with the bathwater.

His first day of term begins with breakfast in the dining hall. The clang of spoons and bowls reverberates to the high walls and vaulted ceiling where house-sized portraits of stern old deans and dons frown down. No lectures for the first week, so he spends the mornings in the library reviewing and deconstructing sacred texts and historical speeches: the Revd. Jonathan Edwards's 'Sinners in the Hands of an Angry God', A. W. Nix's 'Black Diamond Express to Hell', J. C. Burnett's 'The Downfall of Nebuchadnezzar', J. M. Milton's 'Black Camel of Death'.

He makes notes and copies them in his own script so that he might absorb their cadences, muttering certain words to feel the roll of them off his tongue. For here are sermons to set the soul afire, preachers possessed of such terrifying conviction he feels both chastened and inspired.

He explores the books that line the shelves of the seminary's library. He spools through microfiche and reads of radio pioneers like Paul Rader and Charles Fuller and the venerable Theodore Epp. He discovers the roots of evangelism as it originated before Homer and migrated all the way from the cradle of Mesopotamia to the far beyond. Preaching is much more than speaking, he learns, for any man can open his trap and let the breeze blow through it, but only the Holy Spirit can play God's trombone. Yes, every man born must make himself a clear channel, a vessel for the Word.

He learns that language is power, in law, politics, poetry, church or state. A preacher must dominate his congregation the way some folk command animals, for man is like any other beast: sometimes you have to shout to get his ear, sometimes you must pin him down like a snake, or smack him on the nose like a disobedient mutt. But above all a preacher must speak in his own voice, forged of his own experience, for the Holy Spirit is the agent of the original, not the counterfeit, and that is why the Devil is jealous of the Almighty: the Devil is limited to imitation of what is, unable to create what is not. He is a trickster who can throw his voice but never once strike an original note.

One night when he cannot sleep, Enoch summons the courage to go exploring the nocturnal world of the St Mark's campus. Down in the arts and sciences bunker young men with wispy beards tinker with printed circuits and build consoles that look like telephonic switchboards and mutter about Tesla coils and Minimoogs and Léon Theremin. Enoch looks around this subterranean space cluttered with ma-chine parts and is stricken with the creeping-jesus feeling that somewhere a clock is ticking, ticking, ticking away his days, every moment numbered by some all-knowing intelligence.

Before long a bespectacled chap in a combat jacket approaches and asks if it's true Enoch is Frank O'Reilly's son. Enoch says indeed I am, and the young man shakes his head and rubs his face-fuzz and asks so what was it like growing up with the Marconi of Mweelrooney. Enoch is shaken not so much by the question as the young man's awestruck glow.

'How do you know of my father?' he asks.

'His articles in the journals. Your dad was a radical man.'

Enoch can barely remember the old man's face. He has only one photo of his own: Frank standing upon the frozen Rua with a heavily pregnant Kath-leen. Written on the back of the photograph in pencil is the date, December first, 1956, mere days before Enoch was born.

The young man shows him around the bunker. Under his guidance, Enoch familiarises himself with the radio surveillance gear and spends hours with headphones over his ears, surfing through long and shortwave bands, from Minsk to Warsaw, from London to Luxembourg and out into the cosmos it seems, wastelands of static and alien landscapes of whistles and beeps. He asks his bearded friend if, in all his long nights here, he ever heard strange voices on the airwaves, preachers and the like.

'Stay down here long enough,' the young man says, 'and you hear all kinds. The hard part is to stop hearing them.'

When Enoch returns across the quadrangle that night, the stars are arrayed like Morse dots that may or may not portend his fate. He passes through the arched entrance of his dorm and disappears into his room and removes from his suitcase his Philips cassette recorder and his taped copy of *40 Golden Greats*. He sprawls upon his bed and listens to 'Blue Moon' many times before he sleeps.

+ + + + + + + +

At the end of his first week on campus, Enoch receives a letter from his mother. Kathleen will be back

in the country for Frank's anniversary Mass, the sixth
since he passed away. They will have lunch after the
service.

In a small café in Mweelrooney, Kathleen orders
a glass of wine with her salad and downs another
with the main course. The alcohol bestows upon her
cheeks a flush, or maybe it's The Change.

'It was a lovely Mass,' she sighs. 'Father Macken
did your father proud.'

Enoch slurps his burgundy.

'I don't think Dad would have cared much either
way.'

'Don't be ridiculous. Frank was devout.'

'How come he never went to Mass?'

'He was a busy man.'

'He never talked about his work to me.'

Kathleen considers this.

'That was his army training. Your father kept his
own counsel. Not like men today. Yap-yap-yap.'

Enoch takes another slurp of red.

'A fellow in the seminary told me he was published
in the scientific journals.'

'Oh yes. Brains to burn.'

'What happened to his radio equipment?'

'He told me he dumped it all, said it had stopped
working. He was very upset.'

She dabs at her eyes with a napkin.

'Six years gone,' she says. 'I dread coming home. It's hard to be in a house with so many memories.'

'Then put it up for sale.'

Kathleen shrugs.

'I can't let go of it yet.'

She cocks an eyebrow.

'Thinking about your inheritance?'

Before Enoch can reply the waiter arrives with the bill. Kathleen lays a tenner on the table.

'God provides,' she says, then takes her compact from her handbag and checks her reflection.

'Bless us and save us. I look like the wreck of the *Hesperus*.'

'You look fine, mother,' Enoch replies.

Kathleen pats his hand and shoulders her handbag.

'I have a three o' clock boat to catch.'

Enoch sees his mother to the Le Havre ferry bus and there they part, duties discharged for another year. That evening he returns to Ballo Manor and goes through the empty house collecting his last few personal things. When night draws down he finds himself alone in the parlour, shivering with the cold. After a while he rises and prowls the house, pausing at the dusty rug that covers the cellar door. He kicks the rug aside and tugs at the Chubb lock on the door's bolt but it will not give, and no matter how many cupboards he rifles through he cannot find a key.

He goes into the Good Room, which is layered in dust and cluttered with holy relics and trophies, and he begins rooting through drawers packed with his parents' things. At the bottom of a great oak trunk, under layers of pressed flowers and recipes and holy pictures and pendants – Kathleen's bric-a-brac – he finds a postcard depicting rice paddies and pagodas, and a transparent plastic wallet containing a faded photograph of a soldier squinting into the middle distance. Enoch replaces these things in the trunk, and not for the first time or the last, ponders the mystery of the man who sired him.

+ + + + + + + +

Frank O'Reilly's War

1950–1953

The news came in the summer of 1950. The NKPA had invaded South Korea: Seoul had fallen to the Reds. Barely six months off the boat, Frank O'Reilly quit his job as a backroom sparks in Carlo Galliero's Radio & Phonograph Store in the Bronx and surrendered himself to the draft. He was all of twenty-three, an immigrant mick enlisting in the hopes of obtaining citizenship.

Fourteen weeks of rise and shine and roll call, march, chow, inspection, bivouac. He bellied under barbed-wire bales with live rounds whizzing overhead, and when his basic training was complete he could strip and rewire an Arc-5 radio in the time it took to smoke a cigarette. He was ordered to report to Fort Lawton, Washington State, where they issued him with fresh clothing and brand new weapons and injected him with six vaccines.

The Pacific crossing took two weeks. Frank stood

on the deck of the *Marine Phoenix* and watched the waves froth and swell and wondered if his nerve would hold in battle. They docked at Yokohama and made the crossing to Pusan. Then the Kansas Line, the Wyoming Line, the No Name Line, the 38th Parallel. Bed was a blanket and the cold hard ground. Boiled mince on toast was their daily bread – Shit on a Shingle they named it. Men were killed before you learned their names. Some abandoned weapons and ammo and their wounded and just plain bugged out. Some shrugged and fought, they said, because they were told to do so.

Frank served as a Suicide Sam, dispatched to forward observation points. He squinted at a map written in gook and spied on enemy movements and staked out coloured markers and called in clock positions for the pilots to drop their loads. He was a master of scanning radio frequencies, checking for anomalies, devising codes, speaking Irish to confuse the Chinese on the two-way radio. He survived on packs of Camels and C-rations and numbed his nerves with Scotch when the sound of mortar bombardments drilled into the softest part of him, almost exposing nerve and bone. It laid you bare, that sound.

By the end of September they'd breached the Parallel, but a quarter of a million Chinese waited in the hills. Battalions leapfrogged battalions, pushing ever north. The Chinese were invisible and moved by night: dead-eye dicks. They could land a mortar shell in your pocket.

Frank was scouting the high ground over Seoul on the moonlit night the spring offensive hit. Chinese came in waves, the first line armed with hand grenades, the second submachine guns, the third charging empty-handed and just snatching discarded weapons. He was on the horn calling for air support when he heard a millisecond of *shhhheeeow* and a jag of shrapnel tore through his shoulder, then he blacked out from shock or blood loss and re-membered nothing more until he woke in a dark and quiet place.

His first thought was that he was dead, the next was for his boots. Those para boots had kept him alive throughout the winter when other men were dying of frostbite or going home with stumps for feet. Now those boots were gone. His carbine and pistol, gone. He was stretched in his underclothes inside some kind of isolation tank part-filled with slimy water that sloshed and stung his shoulder wound. His brain felt slow and swollen and his body so weak he could barely twitch a limb. He did not know how long he'd been there, and the longer he lay floating in that tepid, salty water the more fear he could feel gathering like fluid in his chest.

He forced himself to quell the claustrophobia, the coffin panic. He visualised radio waves, sine waves, the waveforms of his brain. He remembered stories he'd been taught in school: Oisín in Tír na nÓg, Fionn MacCumhaill and the sacred salmon. Then he pictured images of nicks cut in reindeer bones or mammoth ivory, ancient monuments that could compute the positions of suns and moons.

He remembered Carlo Galliero's gramophones and wax-cylinder machines and heard those cylinders spin. When the stylus touched the wax it released spirits into the ether in the form of songs that told of signs and wonders, of things that had not yet been, things never written down, of meanings in the patterns of birds' migrations and the veins of leaves and ripples in the water. Skits and jokes, riddles and fiddle jigs and Saturday night songs for dancing and Sunday morning songs for mourning, comedy songs and prophecies and vision songs that told of ships sighted in the sky, dragons on the moon.

He imagined music crackling in the cockpits of aircraft passing through the skies over Korea, jamming the Chickasaws' frequencies, wreaking havoc with aviary senses, causing pigeons and gulls and swallows to lose bearings on the earth's magnetic fields. He pictured soundwaves resonating through the farthest precincts of the sky, widening, ever widening, heavenward through the palest blue, through the azure, through the cobalt, into the inky black, causing celestial spheres to hum, casting contrails across the vacuum, speeding through distant meridians.

Then he saw visions on the walls of caves, chains of men descending into a river. For man is born and cries and goes into the grave and is formed again and lifetime piles upon lifetime like sediments in a bog, and all the while the gods look down as taciturn as the moon. The river rises, the river draws back, men flee from it, men run towards it. Men fear the very fire they warm themselves around and recoil from the same death into whose mouth they one day fling themselves, maddened by the babble, speaking in riverish, knowing only riverality, the sound of the river the sound of thought itself, the babble of water that carves out a channel in the mind, erodes the stuff of sanity through repetition, recurring thought patterns or cruel loops like phrases murmured in a fever. And here is the danger for once the rut is cut it becomes easier for subsequent currents generated by the mind to follow these treacherous paths of habit, pulling the thinker of such thoughts down into the cold and murky depths. Because the mind likes those depths, tempts us to climb into the diving bell and lower ourselves to the bottom of our beings, believing that if it gets rough down there we can tug on the line and our saner self our daylight self will haul us back to the shallows. But what if we pull on the line and the line is slack? Our daytime self has abandoned his post. Then comes the horrible sight of a limp line descending to dangle in the current and now we are abandoned and alone anchored to the riverbed in lead-lined boots screaming silently behind the glass knowing no one will come.

But Frank would not succumb. He remembered words he'd read, graffiti scrawled on a wall in Seoul, repeated those words to keep the babble from breaching the walls of his mind:

Brother do not pray for me
Sister do not cry
I was not here
I did not die

+ + + + + + + +

Enoch O'Reilly's Farewell to St Mark's

September 1975

In the second week of September '75, Enoch O'Reilly receives a summons from the Dean of St Mark's, an informal get-to-know-you sort of chat, and when the appointed hour comes round he knocks and enters the office. The Dean looks up from his papers and indicates that Enoch should take a seat. He sets the papers aside and twists the top off a bottle of Cidona and glugs a bit and asks why Enoch chose to enrol in this institution.

Enoch runs his spiel. Six years ago, in the summer months of '69, he heard a preacher on his father's radio and was overcome with the power of the Holy Ghost. Then Elvis came to him in a dream and said go tell it on the mountain, son, at the foot of the Calvary Cross, and all points in between.

The Dean glugs Cidona, his Adam's apple bobbing in his throat.

'Let me get this straight,' he says. 'You believe God

spoke through your father's radio.'

'No sir,' Enoch replies, and before he can stop himself, adds, 'I don't believe in God.'

The Dean takes this in.

'How can you spread the Word of God if you don't believe in Him?'

Enoch thinks fast.

'Because the Word existed first. In the beginning was the Word.'

The Dean frowns and says Enoch should have been born a Pentecostalist. Enoch says a man cannot choose his family, he can only shape his fate. He's babbling now, cannot keep the words from spilling out. He elaborates upon his plans to reinvigorate the clergy and the Church. He was destined to thump the pulpit, he says, to pound the podium, to make that mahogany moan. But he is under no illusions – he must give the people what they want, and what they want is bread and circuses. Mass is the opiate of the religious.

The Dean lights a cigarette and regards Enoch for a moment. Then he turns his eyes to the window and gazes at the cherub fountains in the cobbled quadrangle. A tired-looking man, the Dean. Even his ears seem weary.

'Enoch,' he says eventually, 'I cannot in all

conscience recommend the ordination of a man who says he does not believe in God.'

Enoch examines his knuckles. The air in the room feels curdled.

'I thought this was a progressive university,' he says. 'Not some dogma factory.'

'It is a seminary, sir.' The Dean gets to his feet. 'I must ask you to pack your things and leave.'

'You're making a grave mistake,' Enoch says.

The Dean smiles. It reminds Enoch of an eel.

'My decision is final. Go with God.'

Groggy with shock, Enoch shambles from the office and slowly makes his way across the cobblestones towards his quarters. The next hour he spends pulling shirts and socks from drawers and packing books and tapes. He casts about for anything worth a steal but thinks better of it, then dons his long black coat and hefts his suitcase and skulks from the dormitory, hissing good riddances as he crosses the quadrangle and passes through the gates of St Mark's.

He is bound for Ballo's bus depot, but after that, not a clue. Returning to Mweelrooney would be tantamount to admitting defeat. His mother is abroad again, but if she somehow gets wind he has been expelled from St Mark's she'll undoubtedly dock his allowance. That leaves only the dole office or the boat. He stares at the sticky tarmac beneath his brogues a moment and then strikes out. The way ahead seems to warp and shimmer in the sunlight. He plods, head bowed, through the cloying heat until at last Ballo Harbour rises into view.

As Enoch approaches the bus depot he spies a willowy figure perched upon a mooring pylon on the harbour's woodenworks. A young woman, tall and pale and freckled, auburn hair cut in a geometric bob. She has on a man's suit, low-heeled shoes, and is sipping from a hip flask. On her nose is a pair of wire-rimmed spectacles. She glances up when she hears the clop of Enoch's brogues upon the boardwalk.

'A fellow wanderer,' she says, her voice echoing hours of elocution lessons. 'Thirsty, sir?'

'I could drink the Rua dry.'

She passes the flask and he takes a sip. Scotch. The burn of it is beautiful. The girl shoves over a bit and pats the mooring pylon and asks what brings him here, and Enoch sits and pushes his glasses back on his head and tells her his tale of woe: he entered St Mark's in the hopes of learning more about radio preachers and so on and so forth, but now they've ejected him from the seminary. The girl wrinkles her nose and says if it's any consolation he doesn't look like the holy roller type, to which Enoch replies there's no art to find the mind's construction in the face, Miss –

'Stafford. Alice.'

'O'Reilly, Enoch.'

'Pleased to meet.' She rummages in her bag and applies a dab of lip balm, and already Enoch feels somehow mollified by this young woman's presence. Less clenched or coiled. Maybe it's the Scotch. Alice stands and stretches, stiff and blinking.

'Walk with me a bit.'

They set off northward through the Indian summer afternoon, up the railway tracks that parallel the Rua river. Soon they locate the riverside track that Alice says leads all the way to Murn, and as they walk she explains she's on a day-pass from St Edmund's, the red-brick house. Enoch asks what she did to get committed. Alice says she was never committed, she was admitted of her own accord, but since he asks, she suffered an *episode*. Her father, Professor Charles Stafford, General Consultant, said it was most likely some kind of cathartic event aggravated by overwork, poor diet, lack of sleep and so on, and entrusted her to the care of his colleagues.

'You seem sound enough to me,' says Enoch, and Alice thanks him for the vote of confidence.

A gang of scruffy bullocks draw near, great muscular haunches moving with unlikely fluency. Alice flaps her arms and they rear back chastened. On the far bank piebald ponies shake their manes and stomp their hoofs. A foal, spooked by something, maybe the rumbling intimation of a train, canters for its mother. Two of the ponies break into a gallop and race the length of the meadow.

On they go. It has not rained in many weeks. The fields are prettified with wild carrot and buttercups. You can hear the metallic cackle of a pheasant, the distant crawk of a heron. Mountain ash claws the air, a lady willow trails her fingers in the water.

Alice stops to smell the hawthorn, then crouches to fill her pockets with leaves and flowers, explaining that she will macerate them for preparations for her skin. She points to a yew and tells Enoch of the poisonous leaves used in medicine for killing cancers, and the acacia, and the seed of the fern that if collected at midnight on the night of St John endows the bearer with the gift of invisibility.

'How come you know so much about nature?' he asks.

'My mother,' Alice replies. 'Her garden is a wonder.' She casts her eyes about the river fields.

'We're a conceited species, old flower,' she says.

'We see ourselves in everything, even God. The little bluebells are ten times wiser.'

As she speaks she takes Enoch's hand, but there is nothing untoward about the gesture. They might be schoolchildren on a nature walk. The two fall quiet, walking through the spellbound evening, easy in one another's silence. They pick their steps over cowpats acrawl with horseflies, following the river's wend. Midges hover over the sandbar that forks the current. A pumphouse hums, telegraph wires buzz in harmony. Alice stoops by the river bank and scoops a tiddler from the shallows and cups it in her hands and stares as if engaged in a form of telepathy. Then she sets it free.

'They say the Salmon of Knowledge was spawned in the Rua,' she says. 'So they told us in school.'

The fading sun casts patches of light that might be faerie spells as they pass through a copse of trees. A blackbird sings so sweetly you might never guess its airs are threats against trespass. Up the river a second blackbird replies, then a third resolves the chord.

Many years ago on an island at the mouth of the Sinann, Alice says, there stood around a pool seven slender hazel trees entrusted with the old high magic of the Tuatha Dé Danaan. When the sacred hazel nuts matured they dropped into the pool. But the

Tuatha Dé Danaan hadn't reckoned with the mighty Rua salmon. It found the sacred pool and ate the hazels' kernels, and when it returned to the Rua it glowed.

Alice speaks on about how a druid named Finegas caught the magic salmon and ordered his apprentice Fionn MacCumhaill to cook it on a spit. As Fionn was turning the fish, hot grease scalded his thumb, and he sucked the burn and tasted the knowledge and grew to become a mighty warrior. His last hours were passed on the Rua's banks, and as his spirit left his body, a barge came gliding up the current. Three women in dark robes laid the warrior's body in the boat and covered him with ermine. Some say they took the remains to Tír na nÓg, some say to Tír Faoi Thuinn, some say to a cave in the western cliffs where he sleeps in a crystal coffin until Ireland needs him once again.

As Alice speaks Enoch scans the pale blue heavens tinged with red, and his mind crackles as if picking up transmission from some cosmic source. He thinks of Mesopotamian astronomers transfixed by the positioning of the stars over Babylon, of Mayan or Aztec priests waiting for the return of star chariots bearing the ancients who first populated the earth, interpreting every eclipse as an augury of

Quetzalcoatl or some such celestial head-the-ball's second coming, and he considers all men who beheld the stars before him, Egyptians, Sumerians, Milesians, champions of men looming tall as dolmens in our species' memory.

We are doomed to live in the shadows of such elders, he thinks, burdened with knowing they were as gods before us and we are but runts belittled by their mythic feats. If such giants were set down in the present day, borne by some vessel across the waves of time, their faces would twist with the same disdain Oisín expressed when he returned from Tír na nÓg to see men unable to move a rock from the public road. We have grown weak, thinks Enoch. Compared to the old ones we are less than specks.

But even a speck can regenerate, he supposes. Panspermia fertilises worlds. Words create gods. The universe and its elements, the sun, moon and stars, the mountains and forests and seas and rivers: these are our birthright, our global heredity. The path of a human being's journey is naught but a relearning of all known in the womb, blotted out by the shock of birth, though all our days are numbered.

'We're almost there.'

Alice points to the glass spire of the Rua Hotel's central tower, rising above the trees that ruffle the horizon. A bat flutters about the boughs. They have reached the outskirts of Murn. It is almost fully dark, and Alice looks weary beyond all reckoning.

'Are you all right, Miss Stafford?'

'Tired, old flower. We walked a long way today.'

Scotch in the hotel bar, then they elect to pool their money and take a single room.

'Just in case you get any notions,' Alice says, 'I'm not romantically inclined.' She knocks back a mouthful of Scotch.

Enoch gazes into his tumbler as if looking for impurities.

'Myself, I am betrothed to the Word.'

Alice signals the barman.

'In that case I'm perfectly safe,' she says. 'Let's freshen your drink.'

One more for the road and then up the stairs they go and flop into bed and are soon asleep, top to tail, footsore and spent.

Let us leave them to their rest. When the morning comes Enoch's legs will ache, but those pangs will be eclipsed by the sweetness of their walk, a duet composed of steps and words. Such moments do not last. Alice will be gone, the hip flask on the room's writing desk the only evidence they ever met. Enoch will pick up his suitcase and board a bus out of town, and for eight long years his face will not be seen nor his name spoken in Murn. So let them sleep, peaceful children, while they can.

+ +

IS COMING INTO HER TIME

+ +

re listening to HOLY GHOST RADIO transmitting for your benefit the so

+ +

ERE ARE 2971 DAYS TO THE FLOOD

+ +

+ + + + + + + +

II

THE BROTHERHOOD OF THE FLOOD

+ + + + + + + +

The Why

The river is quiet tonight, but the question still resounds through every quarter of the town. There are no answers, or there are many, dividing, replicating, splitting cells and reproducing. The heart hungers for certainties. Give us falsehood or truth, but answer our plea.

Maybe a man slept too seldom and thought too much. Maybe thoughts of cruel hands on a small boy haunted him into manhood and stole his sleep. Maybe a man did something so unforgivable he could not bear to face his loved ones.

Maybe a man numbed the pain with a little something, but that little something grew until it eclipsed the sun, until he feared he might never breathe the light of another dawn. Maybe a man's beloved did not love him. Maybe a man could not bear how the world had turned pallid, washed out, grey, every day a photocopy of the last. Maybe a man's gesture was misinterpreted and set busy lips gossiping and soon his name was dirt.

Maybe a man's mind burned until the fever of it, the heat of it, turned his soul to char. Maybe a man was not cut out for the work into which he was born and grew sick of the toll, the blood covenant of the farm, the daily tributes to the slaughterhouse god, culling the newborn foal to save the costly mare, the pups in the plastic sack, the stillborn lambs, the myxo hare, the poisoned rat, the savaged sheep, the badger burst and smeared across the back road.

Maybe a man remembered the first night a woman lay with him. The river outside was what he recalled long after he had forgotten her warm breath, the cold sheets, the way they moved together in the darkness and it felt like the first time such a thing had ever happened. And then he heard the river speak, a damnation that at the time had seemed a blessing: *it doesn't get any better than this.* The river's voice stayed with him like a debt that must be honoured no matter what and sometimes when it was quiet he heard it still – had always heard it, like static permeating everything.

He heard it when she told him her period was late, heard it when he shocked her by proposing, heard it over the crying of the kid, the smell of the flat, the shitty nappies, the nights he stayed out late, the screaming in front of the entire street. He heard it the night she threw him out for good and he moved into a two-room tip and was ashamed for the kid to visit, he was still a kid himself who never learned to clean or cook, and there began the drift, the numbness, and he started to believe it when she said it'd be better for everyone if you didn't call around, it only confuses the child, and that's when the darkness came, the sleeping sickness, and as he drank himself blind he remembered what the river said.

Maybe a man lost his job and stared at the walls while his mind ate away his heart, and he lit one cigarette off the last and got under his wife's feet, another child in the house, and no matter how she might reassure him that it's all right, it is not all right, there will never be anything all right about queuing for a handout or a compulsory training course to keep your claim, sat like a child at a desk in a prefab while a man half your age instructs you on how to fill out forms or use the phone.

Maybe a man walked the town remembering the dreams he kindled as a lad before the world shrank to the size of a street and a great weight bore down, and so he disconnected his senses, the pleasure receptors, next stop anhedonia, atrophy, paralysis, self-imposed isolation stemming from hopelessness and what's-the-fucking-use, and now at the worst of it maybe that man succumbs to thoughts of the rope in the haggart, the gun in the shed, or maybe pays a visit to his old sweetheart the Rua, and he descends the steps to stare at her silvery waters and thrust hands into the shallows and wash them clean of the stain of idleness, of entropy. There he teeters on the brink of the tidal extreme and the whoosh and threshing of the weir drowns out voices that might otherwise give pause or call him home.

Maybe the man then steps into the shallows, and though the coldness should shock him to his senses all his wires are down, he is adrift, gone, released from the succession of sickeners his existence has become. Could be he believes he can breathe those waters as his ancestors did. Or maybe he believes nothing. Maybe he is beyond all thought. But this he knows in his blood: should you deliver yourself to the river, the river will not refuse you. The river will take you in.

None of this answers the question why. Such events now seem too small before that question, though they may transcend it in the end. For a man is not defined by his death. Every man has his story, and his life is in the telling.

So we will tell your stories, brothers, one through nine.

+ + + + + + + +

Duine Beath

Our first story begins on an Easter weekend. A boy and his mongrel pup are playing near the entrance to the railroad tunnel that rumbles under the town of Murn. The pup begins to worry at a badger's lair or a rabbit hole. He digs and the boy digs with him and now the ground opens like a grassy mouth. The boy lowers himself into a cave. He strikes a match, and as he casts his eyes around the pit the flame flickers, illuminating images carved into the walls, crude but unmistakable. A human chain: nine men descending into a river.

Word travels and soon experts are called to examine the paintings and translate the runes carved beneath each one. *Duine beath, uisce beatha.* Man-death, water of life. Anthropologists date the drawings to the Palaeolithic era. The cave walls' mineral composition has kept these impressions intact for many centuries, but once exposed to the air they begin to calcify. In time they will degrade completely. Many townsfolk will deny they ever existed

By then the boy is a man who will not live to see his twenty-seventh year.

+ + + + + + + +

Summer's Almost Gone

August 1970

One summer's afternoon when everything looks burnt orange and corduroy brown, the colour of Kodak Instamatic snaps, two boys quit their play by the river and take a shortcut home across the railway tracks. Neither wears a watch, but they know as dogs might that the five o' clock express to Ballo is due, and so they hurry across the sleepers, goaded by the fear of a sprain or a foot stuck under a rail as whistles shrill and train brakes scream.

But not today, thank God. Over they go with all their limbs and down the far slope and into a copse of laurels and blackberry brambles, descending through the shades on a winding narrow path, stealthy as summer ghosts in the undergrowth. Soon they come upon the wreck of a cottage belonging to Bobby Robinson, the doddery old sod with the walking canes and bad stammer who some say is still shell-shocked and keeps a loaded gun ready for German infantry.

Look around: a rusted-out Fiat stands on breeze blocks among clumps of weeds and nettles. A grove of trees is lumped with maggoty crabbers barely worth a steal. The grass is spongy underfoot and sunlight glints off broken jam-jars and jagged cans and there's a smell of rotten cat shit.

The darker-haired lad, an Ellis from Larkin's Park, produces a roll of caps, steals up to the back step and lights a match. He touches the flame to the caproll, which as it falls to the doorstep glows bluely and curls up like a worm. Then he joins his pal – Isaac Miller from across the bridge – where he crouches among the apple trees.

The caps go off, jarringly loud in the balmy afternoon. The back door clatters open and old Bobby Robinson shambles onto the step. He jabs his canes at the smoking, sputtering caproll.

'Blackguards!' he says, squinting into the harsh yellow sunlight as he totters onto the path. The arms of his cardigan are saggy, like loose skin, and give him the appearance of a great slow bat.

The fair-haired lad picks up a crabber and pitches it at the old man. The apple misses but bounces off the car bonnet, and now a threshold has been crossed: an unprovoked attack on a half-deaf coot who never did them a bad hand's turn. Both boys know it, and the old man knows it. The skittish cats and the pitched apple itself know it too, and this prevalent knowing seems to ripple and disrupt the humid air.

The old man swivels his head. 'I'll get the Guards!' he yells, but this is no good at all, for he looks grey-faced and weak and has to lean against the Fiat for support. His canes rattle to the ground and he slides horribly down the bonnet to slump and gasp on the flagstones. His fingers claw feebly at the buttons of his shirt and his face goes the colour of a dried-out beetroot and then of char and the sound that comes from his throat is something a scaldcrow or a daw might make.

The two boys bolt and splash across the stream and back the way they came. They're badly spooked, no doubt about it, their hearts beating like the clappers as they plunge through the brambles, leaves beating their faces and thorns welting their bare arms as they tear up the slope towards the railway tracks.

Now what happens but the five o'clock express comes screaming around the bend, its locomotive maw emitting an earsplitting shriek. The Ellis lad almost lurches into its path but his friend hauls him back. They cringe low and wait for it to pass, then hurry across the humming tracks.

Now all is still. It is the eighteenth of August: somewhere sweethearts are courting beneath a tree, and somewhere a car radio plays Bobbie Gentry, and somewhere in an empty ballroom someone is remembering a day from his childhood such as this, and somewhere else again a stranger steps off a bus and gets the first good look at Murn, and the Rua glides slowly by.

Fringe plastered across his brow, T-shirt confettied with cherry blossoms, the Miller boy gulps air and says, 'We may get our stories straight.' So they crouch at the river's slipway, these scared lads, and tell themselves another version of what has happened, repeat it until the new story is superimposed upon the old. They know it must be close to the truth for the graft to take. If questioned they will say that they walked home through the railway tunnel, which is out of bounds. No matter what, they must stick to the story, even if it turns out the old duffer has suffered a stroke or heart attack.

And as the orange sun ripens they walk to the bridge and go their separate ways, suddenly unwilling to be seen together. The trek home is long, and their evening suppers taste sour and their dreams that night are full of scrabbling canes and shrieking trains and wrinkled apples like screaming babies' faces.

Next morning the two boys meet at the phone box in the Bull Run. Heads or tails, shout, and then young Miller is on the line to Ballo General, says he's a nephew, and now it's a wait of ages until the switchboard lady says Mr Robinson was kept in overnight to recover from an angina attack and discharged that very morning. The boys push out of the phone box weak with relief.

The rest of that month a dead quiet descends upon the town. Not the usual summer's-end stillness when fishermen in thigh-high waders cast their lines across the river's breadth, no, this silence is almost accusatory, an indictment. Now these boys welcome September's approach, because perhaps the autumn gusts will disperse the strange intimation that somehow, in that unnamed season between harvest time and the new school term, something terrible passed between them that might never be redeemed, and in time, sure as winter follows autumn, or a flood torrential rain, something worse might come their way.

+ + + + + + + +

The Carnival Is Over

Easter 1979

Barely has Holy Week begun than the first roust-
about mallets tent pegs into the green, a stake
through the heart of this stodgy old town, and soon
the promenade is transformed into a little city of
stalls and Punch and Judy shows and children's en-
tertainers who conjure poodles from balloons while
the funfair blares Radio Luxembourg.

The Bull Run at the centre of town is thronged
with hawkers, barkers and flim-flam men touting
cheap tapes and jewellery and patterned rugs. Back-
packers establish a bedouin settlement in the shadow
of the handball alley and strum guitars and sing
round campfires into the early hours.

Rumours abound that you can part certain canvas
flaps and see bare-knuckle fights or belly dancers
or whatever your pleasure, and after the long dark
months it's a kind of miracle and summer seems possible once again.

But not for Owen Cody. Come ten o'clock Good Friday morning, this twelve-year-old lad is sat disconsolate and scowling on his own front step, waiting for Brother Crowley's bus to bear him away to some novitiate or convent on the Ballo Horn peninsula for the Easter Retreat. No matter how he's argued with his mum and dad, the fee's been paid and he's going and there's to be no more about it.

Owen tells himself he'll do as bid, repeats this thought right up to the last moment when that big old bus comes a-rolling up the lane. But then something descends upon him, pure fear maybe, the kind that makes you sick, for many's the tale has been told in the schoolyard about Creepy Crowley and how he once broke a boy's jaw for back-answering, and some say he tried to queer another.

The prospect of a weekend alone with a beast like that in a remote kip on the Horn is too much to contemplate. Owen still remembers the day Brother Crowley sidled up to the urinal beside him in the school toilets while he was having a slash. He'll never forget those eyes, cold and dead, the man looking and smelling like a goat that had learned to stand on its trotters. A mob of boys came in and Creepy Crowley zipped up his fork and backed away, but ever after that Owen's suffered nightmares from which he comes awake feeling fingers around his throat, thumbs pressing on his Adam's apple.

There's no way in blazes Owen's getting on that bus, so in a flash of eff-the-consequences he's off and gone. But Crowley's spotted him, he's off the bus and right on Owen's heels, a big man but fit from the handball and the hurling. Owen tears through the Bull Run and down Hill Street towards the bridge and now it's a game of hide-and-seek, hunter stalking quarry, quarry diving into doorways and behind cars, sprinting down the promenade where a sweet breeze hits his face and his ears fill up with fairground sounds.

And here a voice begins to babble in his ear and it's that weird old Rua river, and what does it say only keep on running, son, down the prom where the fair is in full swing and there are punnets of strawberries and cream for sale, and waltzers whirl and the big wheel turns and Wurlitzers hurdy-gurdy-gurdy.

Run, Owen, run into the sideshow stalls, slip nimbly between trailers and hurdle over tow-bars and seek refuge amidst the rumpus that swells to cover your gasps for breath – sweet circus music – the snakecharmer's chanter and the musical saw, the Django gypsy jazz and merry go round calliope sound, old carnival ghosts, spirits of carnies past, pickled twins and djinns and dervishes with henna'd hair and dogfaced wonders and bearded, baldy strongmen. Today these are your friends, son, your guides, so do as they say and hurry where they send you.

Here!

A velvet-curtained entrance, past a hand-painted billboard sign that boasts in Wild West lettering around a backwards-running clock:

MARVIN'S MARVELLOUS
MECHANICAL MUSEUM

Part the drapes and step inside: as your eyes adjust to the dimness they also widen out in wonder. Carny contraptions rescued from Brighton Pier and Coney Island maybe a hundred years ago. Dioramas and daguerreotypes and trick mirrors that as your perspective shifts transform Edwardian gentlemen with waistcoats and waxed moustaches into red-eyed lycanthropes. A carousel of ponies pistoning in time to the rinky-dink saloon tunes pumped out by the gramophone horn mounted on the lid. Owen blinks and looks again: a plaster cast of a two-headed baby. Also zoetropes and Kinetoscopes and animatronic

mannequins with names like Roland the Brain and
Dr Kill-R-Watt. A machine called The Drunkard's
Dream that transforms an old crone into a girdled
blonde bombshell. Coin-operated chambers of horrors and an electric chair with arm-straps and dials
and a sandwich board that says *In this chair over 30
people were electrocuted at Sing Sing Prison, in New
York State 1921–1950s.*

Dazzled by pandemonium, the boy forgets his
wits.

The canvas tent flaps and the red drapes part, admitting blinding light, and when the sunspots clear
he sees, silhouetted there, Creepy Crowley with his
eyes a-blazing. Our boy whirls about, seeking flight,
but Brother Crowley looms with arms outstretched
and Owen yelps as he's lifted clear off the ground
and the voice is a hacksaw rasping, 'YOU LITTLE
MAWK!' and here our story stops without so much
as a stay-tuned or to-be-continued, stops like a clock
or a heartbeat, or grass shocked dead by thunder,
the lapse between peal and flash, the moment when
boyhood ends and whatever is not yet manhood has
begun.

+ + + + + + + +

Charles Stafford's Vision on the Hill

September 1982

When the evenings shorten and shadows draw down, Professor Charles Stafford finds nothing will satisfy him but to roam the fields, out among the moths and bats and foxes, walking the bowers and the byways. Through the dusky light he roves, straying north as far as the Roadstone quarry, west past the sawmill, east to James's Wood, south to the Devil's Elbow.

It was far from such places he was reared. Charlie Stafford came from dirt, the squalor of the Liberties between the wars. He slept in the Phoenix Park and woke to the sounds of horses' clops and the clink of milk bottles and the guttural roar of buses. By day he hid in public toilets from the Black Maria and breathed on his hands to ward off chilblains. He was hungry always, he'd eat anything, crab apples that gave him cramps, berries or mouldy bits of bread, warm candle drippings in the church. At night on

the streets he prayed for a full moon to show itself
and banish the shadows and the ghosts, to protect
him from the old crones who combed their hair and
keened, or child-catchers from the world below. The
moon was a mother watching over him. She promised him a place where there'd be pastries cooking
in the oven. He could smell half moon cakes with
cream.

Jesuits took him in and schooled him and when he
came of age he vowed to repay the fates for his good
fortune. He served as a medic with the Peace Corps
in the Congo first, then the Philippines, then Cam-
bodia. He remembers Ho Chi Minh City, searching
the streets for runaways and strays, *bui doi*, street
kids, kids that lived down sewers. He heard stories
of children killing children, children eating children,
boys who'd been buggered so many times their hearts
had given out. He found an infant girl abandoned
in jungle territory. Her belly was big and tight with
parasites and her skin was yellow from hepatitis and
the doctor said she's dead and Charles Stafford said
she is not dead and blew air up her nose and restored
her breath and carried her back to camp.

Now the Professor comes upon St Cecilia's church
on the hill overlooking Murn, its mighty spire like
a rocket angled at the darkening sky. The door is

unlocked, the interior glimmer-lit by candles. Strange fates befall the best of us, reckons the Professor, that this church's architect Augustus Welby Pugin, a man who cathedralled half the country and designed Westminster Palace, ended up in Bedlam.

Up the aisle he goes, like some groom wedded to his shadow, touching the pews lightly as if to consecrate each one, then he stands for a spell before the altar and turns his eyes towards the West Transept where the baptismal font stands upon its base of Minton tiles, then the golden reredos carved from Caen stone, then in turn the tricolour draped across the left side of the nave. He sees the great oak pulpit and the episcopal seat, the crucified Christ, the central pillars inscribed with the names of all the bishops of Ballo.

When the silence becomes too much the Professor takes his leave of St Cecilia's. On he roves until he gains the summit of Blackberry Hill and there he sits upon the rocks. This hill is soaked with historical blood. The blood of skewered children. The blood of women violated. The blood of turncoats with their throats cut. The blood of rebels who made their stand on a midsummer's night nearly three hundred years ago, slain by balls of lead and grapeshot slung by yeomanry. The blood of Orangemen and their kin cut down by rebels, their bodies mutilated and left for pigs to eat. The blood of the warrior priest Father John Murphy, forty-five years old, strong and agile and bald as an eagle, captured in Tullow ten days after the Rising and charged with committing treason against the British crown, tortured for information, stripped, flogged, hanged and decapitated, his corpse burnt in a barrel of tar and his head impaled on a spike as a warning to those who might be further inspired to martyrdom.

Squatted upon this rock, the Professor looks down upon the town of Murn – a garrison town, a place of blood and iron – and when the breeze quickens and the moon rises on the glinting river he harkens to the whispers of the dead, smells their fetor, senses their phantom outlines, their spirits rising from the waters in a ring-a-rosy of the murdered and the maimed, the raped and piked and burnt. Their ghosts comb the blood-muddy water and when they find their bounty they pass it hand to hand, a reliquary, the severed head of their martyred captain.

And what frightens the Professor is not so much the vision itself but that he feels barely any wonder, little feeling at all. Now come the whispers that insist his faith in some benign guiding hand is foolishness, there's nothing out there in the cosmos but a few

rusty buckets of Sputniks and a NASA satellite wink-
ing like it truly knows the nothingness the world
denies. No higher power nor governing intelligence,
nothing but nature's flux of solar storms and stars
collapsing and even the aurora borealis that glories
over the northern hemisphere is no more than a trick
of the light.

The Professor takes a deep draught of cold, smoky
air and tosses back his head and observes the watching moon, and when at last he descends to the river's
edge he imagines he hears the Rua speak.

+ +

UINE BEATH UISCE BEATHA

+ +

why

+ +

HERE ARE 771 DAYS TO THE FLOOD

+ +

+ + + + + + + +

III

ENOCH O'REILLY AND A TOWN CALLED MURN

+ + + + + + + +

The Prodigal Returns

It is a beautiful August day in 1983 when Enoch
O'Reilly returns to Murn. He is now a man of
twenty-six. Where he's been all these years no one
knows for sure, although anyone who asks is soon
made privy to the details of an odyssey that began
eight autumns ago, back in September of '75. On that
fabled day, says Enoch, he procured passage from
Dublin to Heathrow, Heathrow to Jacksonville Inter-
national, Florida, to make his pilgrimage to the land
of Elvis Presley's birth, and was so bewitched by that
vast and mythic place he stayed for the best part of a
decade.

Now anyone who buys Enoch a drink hears about
years spent in Louisiana, Tennessee, Arkansas and
Kentucky, driving the highways and the byways as
the FM radio blared evangelists whose commitment
to the Spirit and ability to shape a sermon with a
simple system of metaphors – a train ride, a card

game, the seasons – riveted him to the hot pink upholstery of his rented Camaro. They hear tales of Baptist clapboard shack chapels on the edges of cotton fields shaded by chinaberry or cypress trees, and of pastors with voices like mountain lions, and they are subjected to florid descriptions of the taste of watermelon and cinnamon bread on a bayou morning, the smell of magnolia and honeysuckle vine, the glorious sound of white-robed choirs stood waist-deep in river water where suffering souls are born a second time unto the Lord.

But hold your hour, for Enoch's only getting started. By the second drink he reaches the part where he travelled on foot in the homicidal heat to a crossroads somewhere near Charlie's Trace and met a man the living spit of his father, who offered all the riches in this earthly world if he would just accept this key to his cellar. By the fifth drink he'll be recounting his pilgrimage to Sun Studios and feeling so Holy Ghost Radio about the place that he had to calm his spirits with a splurge on a three-hundred-dollar-per-night suite in the Heartbreak Hotel in downtown Memphis.

And yes indeed, he was there in Tennessee that sweltering August night when WMC radio broke the news – the King is dead. How did he react? He reacted by getting blitzed on whiskey. Next morning he woke to find five letters inked on the skin between the first and second knuckle of each digit of his left hand:

D - E - V - I - L

And on the other hand:

E - L - V - I - S

Later after a pint of bourbon he found himself pitting one hand against the other, each trying to best its twin, fingers intertwined like grappling wrestlers' arms or legs, or lovers', or perhaps brothers', Cain and Abel's, the letters all jumbled, ELVISDEVIL and DEVILELVIS, until all meaning dissolved and in shock or grief Enoch saw good in the left hand and evil in the right, and finally he saw the spirit of the King's ghost twin Jesse Garon who had died at birth, whose name Elvis almost carried behind his own – Elvis Aaron Presley – like a shadow shackled to his very self. How the cords stood out on Enoch's forearms as his Devil and Elvis hands struggled for supremacy, each seeming equally pitted, there could be no winner, it was a stalemate that persisted until at last, exhausted from the bout enacted by his two big fists, he slumped on his bed, inky fingers splayed across a pale, unshaven face.

All this time the radio played 'Are You Lonesome

Tonight?', the song newly recast from lover's croon to ghostly hymn. Then the DJ made a solemn vow to play nothing but Elvis Presley songs on every anniversary of his passing (a noble gesture to be sure, but when Enoch tuned in for the following year's anniversary, he says, the rotten liar was playing the Bee Gees).

There and then he decided he would now wear only black, not in honour of the downtrodden and oppressed, as claimed by Johnny Cash, but because it would befit a man in mourning. Those shades of his were now like a widow's veil.

With Elvis dead and gone, Enoch says, he felt again compelled to roam the map, driving aimlessly across the Confederacy, trawling every frequency, monitoring the evangelical stations, senses attuned for the railing cadences he heard on the Holy Ghost Radio ten, twelve, *fourteen* years before. Did he find them? He did not.

Enoch spins all these yarns and more, but those listening might have felt mightily duped if they'd learned that he was not, nor ever had been, in possession of a valid passport. Furthermore, one night during the period he claimed he was in the States, certain locals swear they saw him in the Wicklow hills, bundled up in his frock coat and a scarf that reached his knees, arms outflung and head thrown back like a moonlit scarecrow daring the birds to come perch upon his cruciform. Not to mention reports that one weekend in November 1981 a man fitting his description showed up intoxicated at the Charismatic Communications Convention in the parish hall in Nenagh, claiming he had been booked to deliver a lecture on 'How to Blow God's Trombone', and when informed that he would do no such thing made such a fuss the Charismatics bumrushed him off the premises. Then there were reports of Gardaí being called to apprehend an intoxicated man attempting to gain access to Ballo Manor on the Horn, claiming that his mother had changed the locks and left the country, and when questioned he refused to give a name.

But enough conjecture. This much is for certain: it is a young bull of a man who arrives back in Murn this August day on the three o'clock bus. He stands at six foot one, with massive shoulders and bulging gut. His speaking voice has dropped an octave. He comports himself with a sort of lumbering grace as he pulls his suitcase from the luggage rack and steps into the bus's aisle.

Now something of great significance occurs. The country and western song on the bus's radio fades and a voice announces, *You are listening to Ballo Local Radio, broadcasting from the Marconi Suite of the Rua Hotel*. A sign, Enoch decides. It couldn't be any more a sign than if the bushes on the river bank burst into flame.

The coach's doors swish open and as he descends the steps he registers a shift in the construction of things, as though he can actually feel the town's population increase by a digit. The river seems to glow and sparkle. He removes his tinted glasses and casts his eyes around and breathes in the smells of the warm hay and the vapours of the river. Every tree and flower and blossom and living thing seems to whisper its affirmation.

Yes.

There's something here. The place has changed, or he has changed – he can feel it in his waters. The air crackles with latent energies. He senses secret stores of power. He feels the river's current course in harmony with his blood. He is not at all surprised when he feels himself stiffen in his Y-fronts.

Enoch crosses the bridge and makes a beeline down the promenade towards the Rua Hotel and pushes through the doors and asks the reception clerk to put him through to the studio. The clerk punches a button and hands him the phone.

'Ballo Local.'

'Hello. Is there an opening on your schedule?'

A pause.

'Come on up. Marconi Suite. Room 33.'

Enoch takes a moment, unbuttons his black silk shirt, kisses the chunky rosary around his neck, then goes on up.

The Marconi Suite is a double room partitioned by baffles and glass. A young man with a whiteboy afro sits with his runners up on a desk cluttered with teacups and folders and graphs. His skinny frame is shrink-wrapped in a faded Led Zeppelin T-shirt. He gets to his feet.

'Andy Caffrey at your cervix.'

'Enoch O'Reilly.'

The young man goes for soul brother, Enoch for an orthodox shake. They give up.

'What's with the gravedigger duds?' Caffrey says.

'I wear black in honour of the downtrodden and oppressed.'

'You have radio experience?'

'Five years as chief pastor for the Church of the Holy Ghost Radio, Tennessee.'

Caffrey blinks.

'You might be a little overqualified. We're strictly small time, horse.'

'So was Sun before the King showed up.'

Andy Caffrey chews his lower lip.

'What's your act?'

'*O'Reilly's Revival Hour Live*. A radiophonic Chautauqua tent. I'm here to roar the gospel, sir.'

'What about music?'

'A little bit country, a little bit rock 'n' roll.'

'Live, you said.'

'I need to see the whites of their eyes.'

Caffrey scratches his afro.

'I'll have to run it by the boss-man, Malachy Gordon.'

Caffrey picks up the phone. The phone conversation with Malachy Gordon is brief. Caffrey says *I hear you* a few times and hangs it up and tells Enoch the score: Mr Gordon will consider the proposal. But if Enoch really wants to impress him, Andy confides, he might pitch in and organise this year's church restoration fundraiser, a marathon variety performance known locally as the Holy Show.

A variety performance. Sweet Jesus.

'Count me in,' Enoch says. 'When can we discuss a fee?'

'Right now horse, it's a fee-free situation. At Ballo Local, we do it for love.'

Enoch goes for soul brother, Caffrey for orthodox.

That afternoon Enoch books a room in the Rua Hotel. Rates are cheap, and there's a certain monastic appeal to the hotel life. Travelling salesmen and shamans alike, musicians and itinerant preachers, all must live apart from the mob, unencumbered by the mundanities of rent allowance and smelly drains and mildew on the grouting and lawns in need of mowing, the pesky domesticities that eat away at a great man's sanity.

Yes, thinks Enoch as he gazes from his balcony, here is a dwelling place fit for an apostle of the King. The view of the Rua is singular. This lofty vantage point, a perpetual crane shot of Murn, bestows upon the beholder a feeling of local omniscience. He imagines gazing out on *Wuthering Heights*-type winter nights to see the lights of the town twinkling like fires in a medieval settlement, bisected by that almighty river, under the watchful eye of a feudal lord sequestered in his high castle.

The river weaves and wends and Enoch observes its course. His work here has begun. Some might think a place like Murn inconsequential, but there is no such thing as inconsequence. Miracles can happen in a place like this as easily as in Fatima or Lourdes. Remote though this town might be, he will emblazon its name upon the world's map. He will get the measure of this place and he will master it. He will know the men and he will know their numbers, learn their codes and combinations, and he will learn to play them all. He will build a shining New Jerusalem in this green and peasant land.

Twenty-one miles south of Murn, in the cellar of Ballo Manor, a ghost machine counts down by way of a numerical readout in the top right-hand corner of the monitor screen.

+ + + + 427 DAYS TO THE FLOOD + + + +

+ + + + + + + +

Enoch O'Reilly & the Holy Show

September 1983

A poster on every pillar and pole in Murn.

Enoch O'Reilly is proud to announce:
THE HOLY SHOW
All-day Ballo Local Radio hootenanny at
the Rua Hotel, Sunday, September 9
Proceeds towards the Church
Restoration Fund
Featuring: St Ignatius's School Choir,
Kormac the Kandy Koloured Klown, The
Ballo Céilí Dancers, The Murn Players
and VERY SPECIAL MYSTERY
GUEST
Supper served
12 noon –10 p.m.

And he's off.

Enoch O'Reilly has returned to Murn to manifest

his destiny, to ring them bells and rattle them pots and pans. There burns within his breast the fervour of the seeker, the preacher, the breather of Holy Ghost fire, which it is his sovereign duty to transmit, and by blazes there's not a drop of time to waste. He's up with the sun and out of his hotel room, pounding the roads, rapping on doors, spreading the Word to the working man and the unemployed alike, the housewife and the housebound and the shut-ins squatting fireside in overcoats even in late summer, brooding like exiled Russian devils.

These are a queer people, yes, but still he lingers in their kitchens and eats their porter cake and drinks their too-strong tea and nods at their platitudes and frowns down at their woes. All that canvassing is murder on the feet so Enoch rents a Honda 50, no licence required if you cross the right man's palm, and now he can cover half the diocese before you've had your oats.

All week he can be seen puttering the roads, luxurious hair blowing in the wind, flies kamikazeing themselves on the lenses of his tinted glasses, his frock coat billowing behind him like a warlock's cloak. With Andy Caffrey's help he records a promo trailer and pins a note to the Ballo Local console requesting the other DJs to plug the Holy Show upon

the hour, every hour. He wangles an advertorial feature with the *Ballo Valley Sentinel* and distributes
flyers throughout the parish. He issues scores of little
helpers from the primary schools with sponsorship
cards and ticket books and solicits pledges of money
for spot prizes. On Ballo Local's tab he hires Fran
Gannon the Man with the Van (Every Town Should
Have One) to hype the show through loudspeakers
mounted on his HiAce.

There's no end to Enoch's industry. He charms the
nice ladies from the Novena Society into canvassing
the church gates, and they remark how proud his
mother must be of his good works (Enoch does not
mention that he has no idea where his mother is
upon the globe). He even gets his hands on a CB
radio set and harangues the artic truck drivers until
the shitheels change their wavebands.

Granted, there are times he loses the run of himself. One moment he's flogging raffle tickets outside
Dunne's Stores or in the market square, the next he's
accosting total strangers and shooting his mouth off
about the mystery voice that spoke to him through
the Holy Ghost Radio, about giants on the earth and
rivers of blood and so on and so forth, then he
emerges from a trance to find folk staring strangely
or backing away, and he has to clear his throat and

dispel the awkwardness with a wink or a joke.

At last, on the night before the big event, he convenes a meeting with Andy Caffrey in the ballroom. Enoch tucks his copy of *40 Golden Greats* under his arm and descends the spiral staircase. A quick pow-wow about running order and technical specs then Caffrey rigs up the sound system and as instructed cranks out Elvis at volume so's Enoch can rehearse his special guest star turn, a lively mime-along to 'Jailhouse Rock'.

Seconds into the first run-through Caffrey calls a halt, complaining that Enoch's record sounds more like an Elvis impersonator than the King Himself. He examines the sleeve.

'Thought as much,' he says. 'This is a copycat job.'

Enoch pushes his tinted glasses down his nose and peers over the rims.

'I've had that disc since I was a boy,' he says. 'My mother bought it for me.'

Caffrey nods solemnly.

'My sister got caught out the same with the *Grease* album. Thought she'd got it on the cheap. Halfway through the first song she allowed it sounded different and looked at the cover. *The Pickwick Grease Monkeys*. She bawled her eyes out.' Caffrey runs his finger over the fine print. '"The hits of Elvis, as performed by the Pickwick Presleys." Horse, I can't play this. I'd be laughed right off the station.'

Enoch studies the sleeve more closely now, the garish cartoon Elvis on the front. He remembers 'Are You Lonesome Tonight?' on Radio Luxembourg the night of Elvis's death, how it sounded like a ghost. He examines his mother's inscription – *Little children, keep yourselves from idols* – and wonders if perhaps she was trying to teach him a lesson about the folly of idolatry. Or maybe she was too tight-fisted to pay full price.

Whatever the reason, Caffrey gets his way and a bona fide Elvis album is fetched from the Marconi Suite. It takes about a dozen passes before Enoch is satisfied he can lip-sync every last vocal tic. When the dress rehearsal is over and Caffrey's left, he tucks his copy of the Pickwick Presleys' *40 Golden Greats* under his arm and returns to his hotel room.

+ + + + + + + +

The Holy Show begins at noon. There are clowns and raffles and ball-hopping contests, and between the entertainments Andy Caffrey spins the discs. All afternoon, performers report to reception and collect their laminated VIP passes and ascend the spiral stairs and walk the hall towards the artists' enclosure in the conference room. Enoch can't afford the hotel's catering so he takes care of the spread himself, platters of ham and cheese sandwiches, bowls of Tayto crisps and plastic tubs of takeaway potato salad from Kinsella's Stores. There's Sandeman's port and Hennessy cognac and a full case of Harp and a box of Henri Wintermans cigars.

Enoch works the room, perfecting his most assertive handshake, thanking the artists for their time and talent. By eight o' clock the ballroom is thronged with a motley crowd. Men of enterprise and vision, the kind whose pictures you see in the paper dressed in monkey suits and dickie bows at Knights of Columbanus socials and Lion's Club golf tourneys. Big shots, county councillors, editor of the *Sentinel* Val McCormack, respectable sorts in Sunday dress rubbing shoulders with the common townsfolk and the Teddy boys who commandeer the back rows and put their feet on seats.

Enoch O'Reilly waits in the hotel bar, conserving energy and sipping Scotch, and when his allotted hour draws near he pops out for a calming stroll upon the promenade, his copy of *40 Golden Greats* under his arm. As he walks the river's edge the sounds of the Holy Show's children's choir accompanied by piano chords carry across the peaceful evening. The gentle night holds its breath and the air is laced with smoke, like the residue of some magic show.

Enoch cocks his ear and is very still, and as he listens the children's mingled voices seem to dissolve in the river air and reconstitute as an altogether stranger choir of older, sadder voices and he finds himself contemplating the Rua's ancient sisters, all the rivers of history, the Tiber where Romulus and Remus were set adrift, the Nile that bore Moses away from the murderous Pharaoh in a basket of bulrushes coated with pitch, and the rivers of Babylon and Jordan, and the mighty Mississippi and the holy Ohio and the Yazoo and the mythic Tupelo and the majestic Shenandoah.

He takes a moment to watch the Rua's graceful flow and then descends the slipway to the water's edge, and when he's sure no one is looking he frisbees his old Pickwick Elvis disc into the river. Then he gazes at the river's currents, its tiny whirlpools and its undertows, but try as he might, he cannot divine his future in those sacred whorls.

Enoch emerges from his reverie and dips his hand in the current and blesses himself, and the silver drops cool his cheeks and brow. And now he's ready for the Show.

He wheels about and seems to glide back up the promenade and through the hotel lobby, his feet barely touching the deep pile carpet. Then it's into an empty dressing room where he's stashed his costume in a garment bag. Here the nerves boil and coil in his belly but he commands himself to befriend the fear. Master it, man, or what are you made of?

He unzips the garment bag and removes from the dry-cleaner's gauze a cream-coloured flared jump-suit ordered from a specialist firm whose clientele includes the legendary Randy Rossiter, Ireland's leading Elvis impersonator. The jumpsuit still bears the tart after-scent of chemical cleaning fluids. Enoch's fingers wander over the high collar, the fake rhinestones, the embroidered bell bottoms, the front slashed to the navel in a great brazen V. He works himself into it like a serpent assuming new-grown skin, and it's a bit tight around the chaps right enough, but with any luck it won't split and leave him with his bagpipes hanging out. He pries open a tin of Murray's Supreme Pomade and sculpts his black thatch into a DA the shape of a Cadillac fin and wipes the gunk off his hands with a bandanna that doubles as a shine-rag for his tassled shoes.

A knock on the door. Andy Caffrey pokes his head

inside and says by God that's some get-up, horse. Enoch inquires as to how the day's events have gone. Caffrey says great, great, but he'll have his work cut out after the children's choir, they sang like angels, bless their little hearts. He taps his watch. 'Three minutes to curtain-up.' Then he disappears.

Silence then. Nothing for it but to wait.

Enoch pictures his long-serving copy of *40 Golden Greats* floating down the river like a tiny raft, then his thoughts are scattered by his intro music, Orff's 'O Fortuna'. He'd requested 'Also Sprach Zarathustra', Elvis's traditional entrance fanfare in Vegas, but Caffrey couldn't find a copy and suggested instead the tune from the Old Spice ad.

Enoch dons his tinted glasses and draws himself up to his full six foot one and breathes deeply and gives himself a bit of a wet-dog shake. Down the hall he goes, his heartbeat tolling every step. He mounts the stairs and prowls the wings like a caged animal until 'O Fortuna' has crested its climactic final movement, and then he strides on stage.

The ballroom is packed, every chair taken, the audience three deep at the back. All eyes are on the stage and each second seems charged with more of the present moment than it can rightly hold. Enoch removes the microphone from its stand   Caffrey's cue to drop the needle – and like the forescouts of some approaching cavalry the first chords of 'Jailhouse Rock' pound through the sound system. Enoch snaps into position, legs splayed, knees bent, finger pointing as though identifying some Lee Harvey Oswald in the crowd.

Now behold Elvis in full throat, a fearsome sound, a righteous sound, and Enoch's miming matching him word for word. His lip curls in an evil sneer, he slices the air with karate chops and his knee pumps and his hips shake, and taken by the spirit he stomps his tassled shoes upon the stage.

But what happens next only the impact of his heel upon the floorboards causes the stylus to jump with a lewd ripping sound and now the record's stuck, and as Elvis repeats *let's-rock-let's-rock-let's-rock* like some lobotomy-job, Enoch tries to incorporate the cock-up into his act, miming this idiot mantra *let's-rock-let's-rock-let's-rock* even as he signals to Caffrey to wake the fuck up and pull the plug. When at last he does so a queasy silence consumes the ballroom.

Enoch glances at the microphone in his hand and thumbflicks the switch and there's a loud pop from the PA. For a moment it seems as though he might speak, but he does not speak. A long whistle of feedback.

Now he hears a sound like distant chopper blades, or maybe the *whomp* of herons' wings, and behind that sound a smaller, more insistent sound, like an SOS signal, a sequence of Morse dashes, broadcast from Mweelrooney to Murn. The ticking of a clock, the turning of a dial, a sequence of electromagnetic impulses translated into numbers counting down to catastrophe.

In the audience someone titters. Someone shushes the titterer. Parents, children, schoolteachers, Teddy boys, all crane their necks and gawp.

Oh Enoch, *now* what?

It is the shoes that save him. Yes, the shoes.

Like enchanted taps from a child's fable, those black and tassled brogues strike up a sort of soft-shoe shuffle that within the span of an instant becomes a full-blown tap dance that appears at first preposterous, but only for a moment, because the sound is then picked up by the hall's trick acoustics, generating a Sam Phillips slapback loop of clicks and clacks, by which time those tassels are leaping tongues.

O'Reilly's off and running, boys, he's damn near airborne.

His body bobs like a heavyweight's, he jigs like a blackface minstrel, he hops like a Christian in a pit of serpents and his oily hair flops and his glasses tilt as he flings arms wide in shamanic frenzy, and how else to put it except to say the Holy Ghost, the demon inspiration, the *duende*, the whatever-you-call-it when something primal and primeval comes upon a man and takes possession – this force causes him to leap and spasm, and now the sound of his brogues is hammers beating anvil, no, it's steel wheels on sleepers, that's it, the midnight special, the mystery train, the black diamond express steaming up from Hell and into Paradise with a full complement of saved sinners. And over all this clamour there pours from Enoch's throat a sound that's almost Arabic, a pentatonic wail or call to prayer.

Now the true spirit is upon him and this unheard-of tongue, this *cante jondo*, carries even beyond the walls of the ballroom and into the sacred river night. And lo, the river sings it back on some secret frequency and this only fuels Enoch's engine, drives him on and man alive, he's doing the locomotion. So shake it, brother, shake it, take it to the bridge and bring it on home, and when your long black train pulls in the station step right off and take a bow as the crowd all stand as one. Oh yes, it's a resounding ovation and our Enoch drinks it in, the glory that is his, the sweet wine of acclaim, and he can already see the rave review that will appear in the *Ballo Valley*

Sentinel, with a full-page photograph and a boldface caption: **HOLY SHOWSTOPPER!**

And that, friends, is how Enoch O'Reilly comes into the fullness of his power in the town of Murn in the diocese of Ballo in the autumn of '83. That power may be as of yet unforged and inchoate and freshly smelted, the raw pig-iron of his rearing soul, but it is virile and it is abundant. Like Icarus he has ascended on borrowed wings, like Prometheus he's thieved the stellar fire, and for a glorious moment he knows in his gut and in his marrow and in his balls how it feels to usurp the mighty gods.

+ + + + + + + +

The following is an excerpt from the as yet unaired PBN radio series A Healer's Casebook: interviews with Professor Charles Stafford, *recorded by Bill Howard in the spring of 1984.*

There are those among the more progressive factions of psychiatric treatment who consider Professor Charles Stafford something of a sage. Born in Dublin's Liberties in 1928, he served with the Peace Corps before studying English and Philosophy at UCD, then went on to practise psychiatry in St Patrick's Hospital. After many years spent travelling and lecturing in Europe, Australia and the United States, he accepted the post of Consultant General Psychotherapist in St Edmund's Psychiatric Institution in the southeastern Irish town of Murn in 1966.

The Professor's first book The Common Mind *is due for publication next month. The interview you are about to hear is drawn from sessions*

taped in the Professor's office in St Edmund's, an
expansive room lined with volumes on mythology,
music and anthropology. Our talks ranged over a
wide variety of subjects: philosophy, psychiatry,
art, drawing on case histories that span a twenty-
year career.

**Bill Howard: Professor, why choose now to
publish your first book?**
Charles Stafford: I fell into something of a slump
a couple of years ago. My daughter Alice suggested
I should practise what I preach and write my way
through it.

And did it help?
It did. The mind often seeks to make sense of events
through the imposition of narrative. When you
think of it, the Irish have very little by way of a philo-
sophical canon. We have instead myths, legends, bal-
lads, poems, songs. We prefer to make things up.
Perhaps this is why Mr Freud is reputed to have pro-
nounced us impervious to psychoanalysis. Writing is
no more than the ordering of a system of codified
symbols that we call words, not much more sophist-
icated than cave painting.

But like painting and music, writing is an intuitive

pursuit, originating from the internal organs, the senses, the spleen and the spine, as much as the cerebellum. The soul of art is beyond thought. We do not write books, books write us. We do not 'have' ideas, ideas think us. There's no other way to explain the prophetic nature of so many songs and stories which process the hidden impulses at work in their creators' lives, sort through the evidence, and make eerily accurate prognoses of what will come to pass.

You believe works of art anticipate real events?
Perhaps the creative side of the brain knows what is before us, even as our waking consciousness cannot or will not acknowledge portents of the catastrophes ahead.

You've been quoted as saying that art can be used as an integral component of psychiatric treatment.
Yes. My issue with modern psychiatry is that it views the world only in its own terms. In this case, psychopathology. It treats syndromes rather than individuals. Dosing someone with lithium is not the same as healing them. Anti-psychotics and antidepressants can be an effective part of treatment, but I worry that we're replacing measured analysis and cognitive

therapy with quick-fix pills and powders. The human mind is not some machine that breaks down
periodically. It's an organism, a delicately balanced
ecosystem. All I advocate is that people be given
a chance to take responsibility for their own bodies and minds rather than lining some pharmacist's
pockets. The mind can heal itself through therapy,
creativity, sport, art, meditation. Expression and depression are oppositional impulses.

What brought you here to Murn?
I'm not entirely sure. There are certain places to
which we are all inexplicably drawn. I call them charismatic sites. They radiate a sort of geographical
pull. They might be sacred places, or cursed.

**You once mentioned that on arriving here back in
1966, you sensed a definite pressure in the
atmosphere of the town, an ambient crackle that
you could 'neither place nor name'.**
A man ignores such intuitions at his hazard. The
blood knows things the brain does not. I'm not su-
perstitious, but I felt some sort of tremor. Some cul-
tures believe there is a primal energy at the heart of
the world, and at certain pressure points, where the
earth's skin is thinnest, that energy bubbles up and

bleeds through.

Are you saying Murn is such a site?

It sometimes feels like it. Places can become charged with the personalities of the individuals who have lived there and the events enacted upon their soil. Take a look at Ireland on the map. It looks like an abused child, huddled shivering out there on the west of Europe, beaten and bullied by its bigger siblings, arms extended, seeking solace from across the Atlantic. A caricature perhaps, but caricatures have a way of branding themselves upon a culture's self-perception. Ireland's history is a nightmare of colonial occupation, famine, civil war. Every country has its ghosts, but in order for the patient to be cured of dysfunction, he must at some point detach from the narrative of a troubled past. I believe place and past are the chief factors that shape a human being. I write about this in *The Common Mind*.

Perhaps you might read a passage for us.

This one should do . . .

Half a mile from where I now reside in Murn there once lived a family called Jameson, who owned a distillery by a pond. Annie Jameson of that family married an Italian man, Giuseppe Marconi, and they had

a son, Guglielmo, who grew to become one of the pion-
eers of radio and modern telecommunications.

Some years ago a friend of mine from the Horn Pen-
insula in Ballo, the late Sergeant Frank O'Reilly, an
expert in the field of radio surveillance, drew my atten-
tion to Marconi's hypothesis of immortal sound, which
speculated that there might exist an astral history of
signals which have aged and degraded beyond our hu-
man hearing, but which one day may be Lazarused
back to life through technological advances.

The maestro never built that device, but some of
those ancient voices are preserved in papyrus and
parchment, in bound codices, in Franciscan and
Cistercian libraries. As a boy I lay awake at night
listening to the BBC World Service. Down the road
from where I now live are the origins of the global
apparatus which can now transmit those voices, both
ancient and modern, like a dream or a virus. Be sure
of this: ideas are contagious.

You've quoted Frank O'Reilly several times in the
book. You describe him as one of the most
interesting people you've met.
That's true, although I should make it clear that
Frank was never a patient of mine. He was a friend.

What was so extraordinary about this man?
Frank had a penetrating mind. Something about him reminded me of fishermen from the Horn Peninsula in Ballo where he grew up. A sort of congenital apartness.

What do you mean by that?
They always look as though they have seen over the rim of the world.

What was his main area of expertise?
Surveillance, reconnaissance and intercept techniques. He was fascinated with radios, built his own crystal set when he was a boy.

I believe Frank began his career with the US forces in Korea.
He was a radio operator. He enlisted in 1950 and was discharged in '53.

Is it true he was taken prisoner by the Chinese?
Not exactly. He sustained a shoulder wound in combat and passed out. On regaining consciousness he found himself inside some sort of underground storage tank. He managed to open the tank's hatch and crawl through a sewage pipe, eventually emerging

from a cave in the mountainside. He was in a state of some delirium.

Was he drugged?
I can't say. He described feeling as though his senses had been enhanced or sharpened and he could hear the sounds of insects and birds in incredible detail. Eventually he was spotted and picked up by an American chopper crew. He spent a week in a field hospital, another week in psych.

What was the medical evaluation?
He was diagnosed with combat fatigue. Soon after that he received a letter from the US government offering him an honourable discharge with full benefits if he would comply with repatriation to the country of his birth. He'd been MIA on enemy ground for an unspecified period and was classified a Communist sleeper risk.

I imagine it was hard for him to adjust to civilian life after repatriation.
He used his savings to buy and renovate Ballo Manor on the Horn. He also started an electrical business in Mweelrooney. This was about autumn 1954, I think. He met his wife Kathleen at a dance in the Rua Hotel

ballroom. She was quite religious.

Did Frank share her beliefs?

All Frank really believed in was his work. He led a sort of double life, built a workshop in his cellar and spent hours down there every night. The man's passion was infectious. He could talk for hours about parabolic antennae, field microphones and scanners. He continued to exchange intelligence with army contacts in Cornwall, Northern Australia, Newfoundland, Hawaii, places like that.

And it was then he designed a computerised surveillance device?

He'd been developing the prototype since his return from Korea. He nicknamed it the Hearing Aid. It monitored and indexed radio, satellite, microwave, cellular, fibre-optic and other electromagnetic telecommunications. In other words, telephone calls, telexes, telefaxes, public switched telephone networks and even geostationary satellite transmissions. But for Frank there was a cosmological aspect too.

In what way?

Well, as I mention in the book, Frank was much taken with Marconi's theory of eternal soundwaves, a vision of the universe as a vast repository of faded signals, discontinued index links, that if some day re-animated could allow us to hear Christ's last words on the cross, or the roar of the crowds in the Colosseum, or the first utterances of primordial man, or even the Big Bang itself.

Frank was fond of quoting Marconi's words: 'Every day sees humanity more victorious in the struggle with space and time.' He wanted to pursue the theory of eternal sound to its ultimate end. He conceived of an apparatus that could monitor not just recorded or transmitted sound, but *all* aural emissions down the ages. That was his obsession. And I use that word advisedly.

How did he become interested in flood phenomena?

The Rua river deluged the town of Murn, twenty-odd miles from where he lived, in November 1956. That flood resulted in a series of drownings, then the river froze solid for a week. This happened around the time Frank's son was born. I always suspected the two events were connected in his mind. New parents are particularly sensitive to any threat to their immediate environment.

So that flood had a catalytic effect on Frank?

Yes. He believed it was part of a recurring cycle. In fact, he forecast another flood for November of this year. By the time this programme is broadcast the listener will be able to judge the accuracy of his predictions.

Your book also discusses the subject of suicide clusters recurring in certain locations. Do you have any theories as to what causes these phenomena?

A few, but theories are not answers. The issue is not suicide, it's mental health. Why do people choose the Golden Gate bridge, or throw themselves into the volcano at Mount Mihara? It's hard to generate an open discussion about something like this. There's still too much stigma. To take one's own life is a criminal offence in this country. The church considers it a mortal sin. So no, I can't say for certain why it happens. Nobody can. That's what's so haunting about it. It's a mystery.

[Ends]

+ + + + + + + +

Enoch O'Reilly's *Midnite Special*

September 1983–March 1984

Now in the aftermath of the Holy Show, Enoch O'Reilly briefly attains a sort of fame, or as much fame as a man can lay claim to in a town the size of Murn. For a week or two he is back-slapped in the street, publicans refuse his money, strangers beep the horn and give the thumbs up. And now there is a new element: the womenfolk who approach him on the street or in the Rua Hotel residents' bar with offers to run errands or bring him pot roasts or stewed rhubarb in Tupperware containers, these fragrant ladies nicknamed O'Reilly-ites by the wags at the footrail.

Enoch revels in the attention like a dog might roll in grass. All the world seems for the taking, and who could begrudge the man his hour. So it is something of a suck-in when he receives word that he must serve a period of apprenticeship spinning discs on Ballo Local's graveyard shift before Malachy Gordon will seriously consider his *Revival Hour* proposal.

Enoch swallows his pride and says, yes, it will be his privilege to broadcast to the good townsfolk of Murn, or at least those among the townsfolk still awake.

O'Reilly's *Midnite Special* occupies the midnight–4 a.m. slot. Five nights a week throughout the autumn of '83 and into spring of '84 Enoch rides the mic and mans the decks while Caffrey slots ad cartridges and patches insomniac voices from the incoming calls switchboard. In that cubbyhole of a studio, headphones around his neck, Enoch regales his meagre listenership with a mixum-gatherum of parish news, rambling anecdotes and the occasional gnomic reference to the fire of the Holy Ghost, interspersed with blasts of vintage rockabilly and gospel sounds. The musical policy is strictly oldies. This means no maw-mouthed Mick Jagger music, no bleating Bee Gees nor jungle boogie disco rubbish nor synth-pop jingles, only the rarest and juiciest cuts plundered from Murn and Ballo's thrift shops and car-boot sales. Enoch regards it as his solemn duty to teach the Teddy boys of Murn that there's more to life than the Stray Cats or Showaddy-bloody-waddy.

The Marconi Suite vibrates to the sounds of Elvis Presley, Jerry Lee and Johnny Cash and the Tennessee Three, Roy Orbison, Eddie Cochran, Gene Vincent and his Blue Caps, Buddy Holly and the Crickets, Wanda Jackson, Del Shannon and many others. Rowdy switchblade rockers alternate with tattooed teardrop doo-wop numbers or car-crash sob-a-roonies like Jan and Dean's 'Dead Man's Curve' or Ray Peterson's 'Tell Laura I Love Her' or Stonewall Jackson's 'BJ the DJ', the cautionary tale of a fast-living jock killed in a Georgia auto wreck at the age of twenty-four.

As the wee small hours come a-creeping, Enoch switches to mellower sounds: Luke the Drifter, the Carter Family, the Louvin Brothers. Hunched over the console's green glow, he sips Scotch and nods along to heavenly harmonies and vows not to end up like the other crocks who punch the station's clock. Men like Syl Crosby the breakfast jock, or Dorothy Caulfield, the *Woman's Hour* presenter with a puss on her that'd turn fine wine to vinegar.

And although every moronic request, every hick social function Enoch is obliged to plug inspires black and murderous thoughts, he reads these requests and plugs these events with gusto. Every spare moment is spent hatching scams to impress Malachy Gordon and secure the go-ahead for the *Revival Hour*. Tapes of his graveyard shift are made available for sale in the hotel foyer and at the church gate, three pounds each, proceeds going to charity (none specified). Come spring of '84, after a letter-writing campaign that borders on harassment, his *Midnite Special* is syndicated to seven hospital radio stations throughout the province.

On the night of his St Patrick's special broadcast, Enoch returns to his hotel room, toes off his lucky tassled shoes and sinks into the groaning brown leather sofa and puts his fuming brown stockinged feet up on the matching brown padded footstool and switches on the not exactly brown so much as beigey-grey Panasonic colour television. Balanced on his armrest is a pillow-backed dinner tray on the laminate surface of which sit the remains of his supper (a batterburger-and-onion-rings takeaway combo from Clifford's Fish & Chips, plus a side order of fried bread from the hotel's kitchens). He sips Scotch and stares at the RTÉ test card and soon falls into a peevish sleep.

The night passes fitfully and when the coming dawn sets the room ablaze Enoch wakes and wipes drool from his cheek and stares blearily at the white noise of the television set, and now he frowns and frets over his recent trajectory. The past six months have been a necessary digression, but it cannot go on. That television static calls to mind vague but disturbing stuff about giants on the earth, a flood of waters, rivers turned to blood, and a cold wind blows through the gulf between his night mind and his waking mind, the knowing and not-knowing, and he comes up in a clammy rise of sweat.

His broodings are interrupted by the hysterical bell of the hotel-room phone. Andy Caffrey's on the line.

'Howya, horse,' he says, more than a little drunk.

'It's eight in the bloody morning.'

'I bring good news, big man.'

'Then speak.'

Andy speaks: Malachy Gordon is impressed with how Enoch's handled himself on the graveyard shift for six months straight. *O'Reilly's Revival Hour Live!* has been greenlit for the very next week.

+ +

IME IT IS.

+ +

e killed the oldest son in each family, the flower of youth throughou the land. And he turned their rivers into blood.

+ +

RE 229 DAYS TO THE FLOOD

+ +

+ + + + + + + +

IV

ENOCH O'REILLY'S REVIVAL HOUR

+ + + + + + + +

Enoch O'Reilly & the Hoor of Ballo

Spring–Autumn 1984

Enoch O'Reilly squats cross-legged in his Y-fronts amidst the remains of a Baked Alaska ordered up from room service. His great gut rises and falls as he extends his arms, palms upturned – almost levitating it seems – and he journeys deep within himself to find a state of focus, of total vigilance.

The bedside radio channels news and the television's tuned to Ceefax with the sound turned down. Enoch's eyes swivel like a reptile's surveying the newspapers and magazine cuttings carpeting the floor: reports of three-day weeks and closures and redundancies and national referenda, a crazy-paved collage of the modern world's woes.

Enoch needs a subject for his inaugural *Revival Hour* sermon – not just any subject, mind, but one so scandalous, so sensational, it will strike awe into the heart and soul of every man and woman in Murn, so now he calls upon the deities to zap him with a bolt of inspiration.

His hands reorder the newspaper cuttings, creating random juxtaposings that are damn near eerie. His eyes drink in their sordid tales, scanning for raw material. On page 12 of the *Times* he sees a small report about some new-fangled terror that has New York in a stir.

Enoch examines the article more closely.

He takes up his pen and begins to write.

+ + + + + + + +

Edited transcript of O'Reilly's Revival Hour – Live!
*recorded before a live studio audience on Ballo Local
Radio, March 1984*

Dear friends,

*I stand before you today as the reluctant bearer of
a tale told to me this very morning by an anonymous
caller to Ballo Local, who revealed to me the following
only under assurance of the strictest confidence. After
due examination of my conscience, and consideration
of the public interest, I have elected to repeat what was
revealed to me here in this public forum, while pre-
serving the anonymity of the tale's protagonist. We'll
call him Jimmy.*

*Now, Jimmy had fallen far from grace, poor wretch,
had fallen into idleness and sloth, frequenting the dog
track and the public house and worse. One night as he
staggered home through the dark streets of this town*

he was approached – solicited I should say – by a woman. A woman? Sully not the name of her kind.

This was no fair and fragrant damsel, no more than the black widow or praying mantis. A streetwalker, friends. A man-humping strumpet who lay in wait for her mark, and like a sorceress had produced her box of powders and potions, the dark arts of her vanity case, and transformed herself into Salome, calling not for the sainted head of John the Baptist but the little helmet-head atop the cock-a-doodle-do of the hapless stray that we call . . . Jimmy.

Yes this temptress bedevilled our wayward lad. She lifted her frock and gave him a sniff of the petticoat and took his coin and pulled him into her lair and the poor boy fell, so he did, fell hard and far, down, down, down into the sewer of Hell.

Well friends, you don't need me to blacken my tongue with the details. He lay with the Jezebel. Yes he did. He rattled her pots and pans, is what I'm saying. Cleaned her cobwebs and dusted her clock. He shook her all night long, as the song goes. Then, spent from his toil, he slipped into a fitful sleep beside her.

Hours passed before our Jimmy-boy awoke, drained and droughted from congress with this succubus. He got himself a glass of water and returned to her bed, and aroused perhaps by thoughts of an encore present-

ation, lifted the silk slip from the hoor's haunch. And now the horror, friends, for what does he see inscribed there on the parchment of her rump but a crude tattoo writ in Indian ink. Four characters that fill his Christian heart with as much dread as if he had discovered upon her scalp a trinity of sixes.

What he read was short but it was not sweet. Should any soul among ye be hard of hearing, let me inscribe their shapes in the air with my finger as I sound out their awful vowels.

AY! – for aye, assent, consent, surrender to the basest temptation.

EYE! – for the organ of the beholder, the inlet through which all evil enters.

DEE! – for diabolical, devilish, degenerate.

ESS! – the hissing of the snake that tempted Eve, who corrupted the first among men.

The briefest of all death sentences, four letters long. Say it back to me brothers and sisters. Give me an EH!

[Here the Teddy boys in attendance can be heard to shout: 'EH!']

EYE!

['EYE!']

DEE!

['DEE!']

ESSSS!

['ESSSSSSS!']

The plague, friends. A pestilent agency sent to smote the fornicator, the sodomite, the junkie.

But tell us, I hear you ask, how did the hoor's hide become a canvas? Well, allow your host to speculate. A sailor man put it there, I'd say. Aye, a mariner on shore leave, put to port at the cesspit, the fleshpot of Ballo town, and when this salty dog perhaps learned from his ship's physician that he'd been infected with the she-devil's spoor, the sailor BRANDED her. Just as in times past the unclean were marked and cast out, just as the adulteress was made to wear the scarlet letter on her breast, this mariner tattooed the harpy so that all who came in his wake might be warded off and spared his plight.

But did this deter the hoor?

['NO!']

Did she get her to a nunnery?

['NO!']

Did she continue to ply her trade?

['N-YES!']

Aye. She sloped upriver to Murn and brought to us a pox. A PLAGUE, my brothers and sisters, here among our number.

Beware, young men of Murn. The she-wolf walks the night. She will wait until you have taken drink and slink in for the mount. She will suck from you the breath of life, not from your mouth with her mouth, but from your loins – the very cradle of nature's production – with her own putrid loins, the forked tongue of her sex, the fetid delta in which so many a young man's issue hath drowned.

So I beg of you to be chaste. Let the story of poor Jimmy serve as a caution to those who would indulge in the itch for which there is no prudent scratch. For let it be recorded, this young man paid way too high a price for a simple rattle of the bones.

Here endeth this sorry tale of a seed-sowing which became a reaping, yea, by the scythe of Death itself.

The phone at Ballo Local starts ringing off the hook almost as soon as the inaugural *Revival Hour* is wrapped, panicked folk demanding to be told details of the horrible plague the man on the radio was raving on about, where to get inoculated, will it be covered by the medical card. Local journalists, gobsmacked at his audacity, demand that Enoch divulge his sources.

Enoch doesn't know what to tell them. He made the whole thing up. But now the story's been syndicated to every paper in the Hibernian Ink Publishing Group and even warrants a few columns in the

Enquirer. The *Sunday World* puts him on page 3 with the headline 'Shock Jock Causes Panic in Murn'. The *Sentinel* runs a horrified editorial.

Enoch holes up in his hotel room and waits for the controversy to blow itself out. Then one evening the bedside telephone rings. He picks it up and Andy Caffrey's on the line conveying Malachy's warmest congratulations: the *Revival Hour* repeat generated record listening figures. The slot's been moved to Saturday night. It's a hit.

Enoch feels the warm surge of approbation. No, of triumph. At last the recognition he has craved. But as the hot flushes of elation begin to cool, he ponders his predicament. A man catches lightning on his first attempt. How the hell is he supposed to follow that?

The answer is quite simple: with more of the same. Throughout the spring and summer and autumn of 1984, weekend after weekend, Enoch outdoes himself with efforts to make each *Revival Hour* broadcast more controversial than the last. In late April, when he hears stats stating that '83 was a record year for Irish lassies boarding the boat for London to terminate their pregnancies, he composes a written request to the Department of Education which secures a copy of one of those abortion horror films the nuns use to scare their charges into chastity. On receipt of the print Enoch heads straight to Rafferty's cinema and pays the projectionist a tenner to snip a forty-five-second segment from the grisliest scene and fashion it into a recurring loop. He then borrows St Ignatius's School's projector and screen. Andy Caffrey has a brainstorm and volunteers the Alice Cooper LP the 'Dead Babies' song appears on.

The *Revival Hour Abortion Special* is subsequently described by a doesn't-half-fancy-himself reporter from *Hot Press* magazine as 'an act of Situationist art terrorism'. It isn't just the images projected on the screen, nor the subtitles that describe in detail how murdering quacks douse embryos with acid and methodically dismember them and hoover out the parts. Nor is it Alice's infanticidal little number blaring at high volume. No, it's the Grand Guignol frenzy into which Enoch whips himself as he holds aloft a Cabbage Patch doll and violates it with a coat hanger while novelty-shop blood spurts from its eyes.

Such shenanigans polarise the people of Murn. For every fan letter that arrives at Ballo Local, there are two or three items of hate mail. One grim afternoon a Novena Society lady berates Enoch on the street, asking him to spare a thought for his mother, for the poor woman must be mortified at his carry-on, and Enoch has to bite back a retort about

Kathleen most likely sunning herself near some grotto in the south of France, far from the reach of Ballo Local's transmitter.

Soon after that he receives a call from the parish priest Father John Callaghan, who suggests meeting for a drink at the hotel bar. Against his better judgement, Enoch agrees. The priest gives him a royal roasting, calling him an embarrassment to Murn and accusing him of using the trappings of ministry for the sake of scaremongering and peddling filth. 'It's a form of simony,' says Father Callaghan, 'and it has to stop.'

But the *Revival Hour*s keep on coming. In May, Enoch links the desecration of Kilcody graveyard to a (completely fictional) local Satanic cult. Come June he delivers a monologue which alleges a prominent member of Murn Town Council is selling snuff films from the back of his van. In July he claims to have seen Elvis's twin Jesse alive and well and running a kennels in Mweelrooney. August finds him raving on about naked mud-wrestling tournaments taking place after dark at the Roadstone quarry.

By now the *Revival Hour* has achieved regional notoriety, but the strain begins to takes its toll. Seldom does Enoch sleep after a show. Too wired. The most he can manage is an hour or two before an attack of the heebie-jeebies jerks him awake and he has to deep-breathe to keep from hyperventilating. He coins a name for this affliction: The Claw of Death. It is a feeling like a slow heart seizure, brought on by the awful sense that time is somehow running out.

It is now September of '84, and he's attained the grand old age of twenty-seven. Most nights he paces his hotel room, mood elevatoring, sick of the sound of his own voice, nagged by the feeling that he's somehow lost his way, become a Vegas parody of himself, a cheap controversialist, publicity hound, performing seal.

Enoch's ponderings grow bleaker. His mother has abandoned Ballo Manor to the cobwebs, flitting from basilica to basilica on the old man's savings and insurance money, leaving her son to contend with that Dad-shaped hole. Aye, Frank is croaked all right, but sometimes it feels as if the old man's ghost is haunting him, sucking all his blood, burdening him with judgements he can barely comprehend, the sins of the father handed down, the sound of wings over the river, that eerie old river Enoch hears from his hotel window every night as he falls asleep.

At last he wearies of these maunderings and, as if to cleanse himself of their residue, peels off his clothes and steps into the shower stall and allows the scalding water to wash over his skin until he is flushed and pink. He wraps a towel around his prodigious middle and laces his rosary around his neck and splashes Old Spice on his face and chest hair. He stares at the mirror and asks his reflection has it come to this, Enoch O'Reilly a circus geek, and his reflection responds it most certainly has, old son, now what are you going to do about it?

Pour a Scotch, is what. He takes his glass out onto the balcony of his hotel room and beholds the Rua river, hears the whispering of the current as it hustles south. He has strayed far from the path, she tells him, but a man can always change his ways. He must find his way back to the source. He must begin again, anew, in his search for the power of the Word.

Now, struck by a sudden thought, scraps of language gathering in his mind, he sets down his glass and hurries inside to his writing desk. So watch, friends, as the nib of his pen begins to move across the paper, operating of its own accord, it seems, transcribing the river's music, her babble, her lullaby. All night and into the morning he writes, rewrites, drafts, redrafts, circling and recircling a central theme. The coming week will pass like a fever dream as Enoch is called from sleep again and again to channel the sounds of the river. Soon folk will cross the road to avoid him, or finish up their drinks when he enters the pub, fearful that he will grab their arm, wired and wild-eyed and babbling have you heard it mister, the Rua's music, his uncanny eyes making men pat for their wallets and women finger buttons on their blouses.

No, he will not bathe nor rest until his work is done. His next sermon will be his finest yet. The finished manuscript will run to some thirty-five foolscap pages, which he will then cut and shape over a feverish weekend of industry. There will be no more cheap gimmicks, no more bread and circuses. Enoch O'Reilly has been reborn with a poet's heart.

+ +

AY AWAY FROM THE RIVER

+ +

giants on the earth in ancient days. The sons of God came unto the daughters of men, and they bore children to them, and the same became

mighty men which were of old, men of renown. And God saw that the

+ +

AYS TO THE FLOOD

+ +

+ + + + + + + +

V

THE BROTHERHOOD OF THE FLOOD

+ + + + + + + +

Iggy Ellis & the Fire

Late Summer 1984

If Iggy Ellis had stuck it out for one more week, a day even, he might have heeded the tiny voices that beseeched him not to do it, endure another hour, brother, and then another hour yet, if you gut it out you'll be all right. But no man can perceive the depth or duration of the blackness that consumes him. Only when he has crossed the threshold that partitions this world from the next can he look back with the perfect perspective of the dead.

It was in the muggy summer of 1984 that Iggy Ellis was released into the community from St Edmund's Psychiatric Hospital to take a post as caretaker and security guard at New Larkin Park, the new council estate under construction on the edge of Murn. They gave him a battery-powered torch and a second-hand walkie-talkie and lodged him in the caretaker's residence.

The other houses were as yet unoccupied pending

council list allocations. As part of an incentive deal
to attract first-time tenants, the oil tanks were to be
half-filled free of charge and the lawns freshly mown.
Iggy didn't mind the work but he missed his meals,
his bed, the familiar sounds and smells of St Edmund's, and he missed watching the nurses throw
bread spiked with Largactyl to the gulls and taking bets on which one would fly the farthest. Here
in this empty estate the least thing made him frail:
the crackling of his walkie-talkie, wind shrieking in
the chimney, stray dogs sniffing and shitting on the
green. He drank himself to sleep and woke in the
mornings wincing from the effects of gin or whiskey.

Some caretaker he'd turned out to be: his own kitchen reeked of rot and the linoleum needed a good
scrub and there were scummy teacups all over the
shop. Dead fruit flies carpeted the table and the ba-
nanas in the bowl were black, and he was afraid to go
near the bin since he'd dumped a pound of gone-off
mince a week ago.

One morning he heard the first post hitting the
doormat with the sound of cow dung splattering
tarmacadam. Among the flyers and freesheets was
a letter from the council informing Iggy that the
first residents of New Larkin Park would soon be
moving in. Iggy binned the letter and went drinking

at the Island Inn where a man played a Casio key-
board and sang country songs. 'Jambalaya' echoed
through his mind as he shambled home.

Later he sat elbowed over his kitchen table and
placed a cigarette between his lips and flicked his
lighter and observed the stem of the flame undu-
lating like a belly dancer's body. He pondered the
coming of Hallowe'en, fireworks flowering across the
sky, bangers and hummers and Catherine wheels.
The imminent arrival of the residents filled his heart
with dread. He feared that they would label him a
schizo from the mentaller, warn their children away
from him, spread lies and make of him a bogeyman,
a golem. He saw them conspiring on the green like
packs of rats or jackals, circulating his mugshot and
branding him a flasher or a sex maniac. Let them
come, he thought, let them come, they can fucking
nuke the place for all I care. Let them shriek through
megaphones: Iggy we know you're in there, Iggy we
know you're armed, Iggy come quietly and we'll see
you get a fair old shake. Damn their piggy little eyes,
and if they've piggy little children, then damn their
eyes as well.

Iggy poured another nightcap and now for some
unknown reason all he could think of was what his
father used to say when his mother asked what he'd

do if he won the sweepstakes. *Go mad and paint my arse black*, the old man said.

Iggy went rooting in his cupboards until he found a tin of black emulsion among the cans of woodstain and turpentine. He doused his fag and then stripped off and plucked a paint brush from where it stewed in a jar of white spirit, stared blearily at it for a moment and began to paint himself. He did not stop until his hide was black as a Moor's. Then out he went into the night, the itching, drying paint like a new-grown pelt stretched tightly upon his bones.

Who knows how long it took to strip the front rooms of their curtains, to knot the fabric into a daisy-chain of rope, to douse those curtains with fuel siphoned from the tanks at the back of each dwelling, and to use the rope to link the tanks. But when Iggy's work was done he lit another cigarette, and when that cigarette was burned down to the brand he touched it to the tail of this enormous fuse he'd fashioned. The flame took fast. Iggy stalked out of the estate and cut across the fields, his eyes and teeth the only parts of him that could be seen.

He did not flinch as the first *whomp* tore through the night, nor as windows shattered from the heat, nor as the smoke billowed into the sky, nor as the reek of melting garden furniture soured the air. On he walked across the waving meadows, his path backlit by roaring, crackling flames, and when at last he'd put the snoozing town behind him and scaled the slope of Blackberry Hill, he sat upon its summit and watched the inferno glow and roar on the edge of Murn, and faith it was a fair old sight, orange tongues illuminating a backdrop of dumbstruck mountains.

He watched New Larkin Park burn for an hour or more and then his shadow-form merged with the night, and by all accounts he was neither seen nor heard tell of again until the time of the flood.

+ + + + + + + +

The Sin Eaters & Billy Litt

Early September 1984

A gom of a moon looks down as Billy Litt locks the gate to Carbury's Abattoir and stands sucking on a Sweet Afton and looking asquint at the shivering waters. He is wiry and sort of spring-loaded, with black unruly hair and a hint of flint in the eye that would remind you of the ruthless way he used to drive drill-bit through punch-mark on those rectangular plates in engineering class, or worked the lathe, or hammered iron in the forge.

Now on this moonlit night he looks at his shadow on the path under the orange streetlight and wonders in his way if that shadow is cast by the man or if the man is the shadow of the darkness cast, but such wonderings get him nowhere but bamboozled. He stamps his feet and swings and thumps his arms to beat out the cold. He has on a donkey jacket over a hooded Adidas sweatshirt and his jeans and boots are streaked with muck and he wears his lucky rabbit's foot around his neck. One time the foreman asked if that thing is cured and Billy said sure it's dead and the foreman slapped his arm and said he should be on the telly.

Five short years Billy's been yard man at Carbury's Abattoir, contracted in turn to Ballo Valley Meats & Poultry Produce. The man from AnCO got him the job and now there's not a thing he doesn't know about the ways of pigs. He knows when they see the prod their squeals are almost human-like because they well enough smell their fate: captive bolt to the head, then strung by the hind leg above the killing floor, then a butcher's knife across the throat, main artery slit, drain the blood. Then down the piggy comes, pullers tear off the hide, out with the guts and check for parasites, the head goes on a hook and gets winched to the top rack for inspection and then they split the carcass into sides. One of Billy's special jobs is to dump the offal in the river after hours, a little extra in his pay for keeping schtum.

Billy Litt was born to do this work. His father first took him here when the abattoir was no more than a shed. Billy was made to stand outside while the old man went in for dogmeat. He pottered about in the dirt and then he heard a shot and a great loud moan, then another shot and a thump went through the flagstones. It was all over in a minute, but he never forgot that sound. Sometimes he hears it in his sleep, can feel the mighty heft of that pop-gun in his hands. He imagines what a hoot it would be to travel back in time and plug the little shits in school who called him names and treated him like a leper because of his condition.

Young Billy was covered with so many warts he looked like something from a comic book. No amount of Compound W would effect a cure. This affliction got so bad his mother took him to see the healer woman and the healer woman bought the warts for a penny and told Billy to put the coin under his pillow and in a day or two they'd be gone. It worked and all, but the lads in school still called him vicious names. They said he was an eyesore, a freak, the abortion that got away.

Billy draws deep on his cigarette, droughted after the long day's work. A pint of cider would go down sweet, a couple even sweeter. About now in the Spoke Tom the barman would be squinting at the television mounted over the bottles of spirits, arms folded, tea-towel slung over his shoulder, watching the late-night horror shows, something like *Salem's Lot*, with that vampire floating outside the sleeping boy's bedroom scratching the windows and wanting to be let in, but sure everyone knows a vampire can't cross your threshold unless you ask.

Mostly Billy spends his nights in the Spoke pumping coins into the jukebox and playing himself at pool. He likes it there. He likes the rumble and roll of the ball into the pool table's innards. He likes the music that blares from the jukebox and the way the Schweppes crates are stacked by the public phone. He likes the loading yard where they store the kegs. Most of all he likes the girls that sit and chatter there like sparrows. Not the fierce-looking bints with dyed hair and docker's arms, rough as any man, but the younger ones with the bangles and dangly earrings and pedal pushers.

Billy never had luck with the birds. Jacqueline Dagg asked him on a walk once and he went beetroot but he said all right. They strolled the prom and sat on a bench and he didn't know where to look, and maybe she only done it for a bet, because after a time she just snorted and got up and left, but that wasn't near the end of it. She told untruths around the town. She said he pulled his mickey out and it was covered in warts but that was a black lie – Billy's mickey was about the only part of him that was never afflicted. But word went through Murn like a dose and isn't that the way of things, a lie that cheats its passage travels faster than the poor old pauper truth.

Billy contemplates revenge on his former tor-
mentors. He'd have to be sly about it, choose the
mark and slip a pig tranquilliser into his drink and
bring him somewhere quiet, maybe the handball alley, set him down among the Coke cans and the dog
shit and fag butts, tie a plastic bag over the head and
an elastic band around the neck, the bag inflating
and deflating like a funny-looking fish.

Who's the freak now, fish-face?

The hard part would be the body. The river would
be too chancy. The corpse might wash up. You'd have
to feed it to the pigs. Their leavings wouldn't fill a
slops bucket, a few teeth maybe. It could be done.
He has the keys. It's a long weekend. The pigs go
to slaughter Tuesday morning, bacon for the winter,
and didn't there used to be a man whose job it was
to swallow all the badness of people who died in the
town? The Sin Eater he was called. It would be just
like that. The pigs eat the body, the people eat the
pigs and the sins of the man and that's the way the
world goes round.

Footsteps on the quay. Someone's coming up the
bank. Billy squints into the night. A lanky-looking
dork in a three-piece suit. The dork stops down the
river a bit and gazes into the water. What's he looking
at? Admiring his reflection, his fine-cut pinstripes.

That suit would look good on Billy. Maybe he should waylay the dork and do the plastic bag trick and swap clothes and dump the body in the river and everyone would think the floater was him. He could take on a new identity and move to a town where no one would call him names or remember when he was covered in warts. That suit would be like an invisibility cloak. He could sign on in every county. When the man on the new claims hatch asked his name he'd put on a traveller's accent and say, Ger Connors boss. There must be millions of travellers named Ger Connors, he'd never get caught. Then when the claims came through he could book passage on the ferry and once out of the harbour he would climb to the top deck and lean over the rails and look back at Murn and spit and bid good riddance.

Billy fingers his rabbit's foot. The dork's finished looking at himself in the river and now he's coming up the quay. Billy tosses his cigarette and nods g'mora. The dork nods back.

'Might rain,' he says in passing.

Billy pictures him crumpled in the gutter, a Lipton's bag over his head.

'Let it,' he says and draws up his hood.

+ + + + + + + +

Lights Out for Nicky

Early October 1984

Fog swells from the river and swirls across the prom and up the gasyard lane and through the twistyturny streets of Murn, its tendrils seeping under doorjambs and down chimney flues and inseminating sleep with whispers, vapours, the vapours, an insidious melancholia that obscures the mind.

So come and enter the murk that transforms Murn into a damp dream of itself and makes familiar buildings loom like the prows of trawlers come aground. Listen hard and you'll discern the lowing of the foghorn at Ballo Lighthouse answering the plaintive bell of St Cecilia's, and as we walk this mist becomes the mist of other mornings, long-ago mornings, when streetlights glow wanly through the murk as we are sucked schoolward down the Coalyard Road, where phantom figures move through these banks of fog, monks at vespers, and all footsteps and morning salutations are amplified by the saturated air.

On we drift through the gates of the Juniorate, down the hall and in the open door of Rang 5B where the Fifth Years get out their Civics books. The room hums with monkey chatter and spitballs and knuckles tournaments while the boys wait for a teacher to appear.

Back there by the window Owen Cody gazes across the shrouded school garden at willows that wilt over young shrubs as if to bestow upon them sad maternal kisses. He tilts his chair and sketches in his copy the cracks in the ceiling and sees inscribed in the plaster there a rough map of the Rua and her sister tributaries, which become tree branches, which become cracks again, and he wonders how deep those fissures go, and if Heaven might ever fall.

Across the aisle sits Nicky Wickham, the cuffs of his denim jacket crusted with dry patches of Tippex like snail trails or white snot. Feet up on the desk, he picks his nose and flips through this week's *Sounds*. Nicky's been prone to blackouts since he was in short trousers. When he takes fit the teacher present can only lever a wooden spoon between his teeth to prevent him biting or swallowing his tongue, turn him on his side and call his mother.

Fifteen or twenty minutes pass before Enoch O'Reilly appears in the doorway and the boys' clatter and noise diminuendos into coughs and whispers.

The students get a good eyeball-full as he slams the door and stomps across the room and places a leather briefcase on the teacher's desk. His sleeves are rolled up to the elbow, exposing thick hams of forearms, and his tinted glasses are perched on his head like a hairband. The black silk shirt is open to the breastbone, a chunky rosary nestled against his chest. His skin is that of a young enough man, but something in his bearing seems very old, and as he introduces himself the realisation dawns across the room that this is the man their parents and the priest have been giving out about, the one with the weekly radio show, and somehow he's wangled his way into their Civics class.

I don't know why she swallowed a fly – for some reason Owen thinks of this line from the children's song as he stares at O'Reilly's shiny tassled shoes. He can imagine them clopping across the floor of a dancehall as if in an old film with crackly music: ghost ladies and ghost gents in tuxedos and ballgowns applauding around the perimeter of polished tiles as the owner of those shoes waltzes a dead-eyed mannequin across the boards, the netting of its wedding veil swishing like a great white cobweb . . .

Enoch wipes a Venn diagram from the blackboard and chalks his name up in jagged capitals and rubs dust from his fingers. The backbenchers seem to sense his distraction and start to fidget and murmur, so what does Enoch do only stand right up on one of the front desks like a prophet on a mountain peak, his complexion the colour of corned beef. SILENCE! he roars, and the air itself appears to quiver.

From the atlas-charted walls to the gumstuck radiators he scans the room. Not one boy dares make a sound. Enoch frowns at the chalk dust he's wiped across his tight black trousers and fetches his briefcase and cracks it open and takes from it a sheaf of papers.

'Broadcasting,' he says, 'is the art of blowing God's trombone.'

Owen puts up his hand.

'What?' snaps Enoch.

'Sir, Nicky's taken fit.'

The entire class swivels around and sure enough Nicky Wickham's eyes are rolled back in his head and his *Sounds* is scrunched up in his fingers. Owen grabs a duffler from its hook and spreads it on the floor to lie Nicky down on. One of the other boys swipes the wooden spoon from the teacher's desk and then it's baton-relayed all the way to Owen, who after some exploration levers the spoon handle until it's fixed between Nicky's teeth.

Enoch watches this with a curious detachment,

then slowly makes his way down the aisle and gazes down at Nicky, who is trembling something sorrowful – there might be tiny moths trapped behind his eyelids. Enoch crouches and snaps fingers in front of Nicky's face like a metronome, once, twice, three times. The room goes quiet. Four, five, six, and Enoch says, 'Lazarus, come out,' like that, and on the ninth beat – Owen counts them – Nicky's eyes flutter open, silvery with tears, and he begins to babble, words tumbling from his throat:

'Everything that is in the earth shall die,' he says. 'He will turn their rivers to blood.'

+ +

IVER KNOWS WHAT TIME IT IS

+ +

n the month of Neverember in a town by the river you had nothing to giv

+ +

HERE ARE 26 DAYS TO THE FLOOD

+ +

+ + + + + + + +

VI

THE RIVER AND ENOCH O'REILLY

+ + + + + + + +

No More Bread & Circuses

October 1984, in the weeks before the Flood

On a Saturday evening in mid-October, Enoch O'Reilly slugs down a mug of malt-fortified tea and descends to the ballroom for a new kind of *Revival Hour*. He barely eats a bite in the lapse between soundcheck and showtime, and instead sits in a quiet corner of the Rua Hotel bar sipping Glenfiddich and conserving energy. His fingernails are bitten to the quick, his hair is dirty and his shirt reeks of sweat and his eyes roll a little in their sockets, but his tassled shoes look shiny as new.

Folk begin filing in at 7.30. Enoch paces the stage's wings muttering and shuffling his papers and re-reading certain passages of his monologue, which marks something of a radical change in style. Something within him now baulks at shock-horror Old Testament screeds or mountain-top jeremiads. In preparation for tonight's performance he's been reviewing videotapes of the Pope's Irish visit from five years back. The Phoenix Park was bedecked with banners sixty feet high, emblazoned with the papal coat of arms, sewn together by hundreds of nuns from convents around the country. All of Dublin, even Mountjoy Jail, was decorated yellow and white. The radio played Polish folk dances. A million people gathered for the Papal Mass singing 'He's Got the Whole World in His Hands'. His Holiness was in full battle dress, his voice solemn and warm as he delivered the words that would become a national catchphrase and adorn the cover of a best-selling LP, words set free over the heads of the Galway tribes like rare butterflies or white doves that would live forever, repeated through the various media:

'*Young people of Ireland . . . I love you.*'

Seven words that made Ireland swoon.

Straight-faced sincerity, Enoch decides – *that's* the way to go. Tonight he'll contribute something of substance to the world, a work of art perhaps, of poetry, perfect aesthetic form. For tonight's broadcast he'll employ that subtlest of forms, the pastoral homily. The subject: the Rua herself, the town's greatest feature and most enduring presence. The words he will speak are scarcely his – they were whispered to him by the river.

A few minutes before showtime he risks a peek through the curtains. The hall is jammed with rubberneckers and local reporters, Teddy boys and respectable folk alike. They look, Enoch thinks, like baby birds awaiting worms. At the back of the ballroom, beside the gratuity table laden with teapots and plates of cheese-and-coleslaw sandwiches, Andy Caffrey hunches over the sound and lighting boards.

On the dot of eight the red light on the console glows as the needle drops on the old Albert E. Brumley composition 'Heaven's Radio Station Is on the Air'. A five-fingered countdown cues the fade, then Enoch O'Reilly strides on stage, his now slightly tatty frock coat flapping at the backs of his knees like a boxer's robe. His tinted glasses are in place and his stained black silk shirt is unbuttoned to the sternum, exposing his rosary. His shoes reflect the footlights as he approaches the microphone and commences to speak.

'Behold,' he says, 'I have received commandment to bless, and I cannot reverse it.'

In the back row Teddy boys glance at each other, eyebrows raised. They are unaware that these words, a quotation from Numbers, were among those transmitted by Samuel Morse via a telegraph demonstration line from Washington to Baltimore on 24 May 1844 – the first recorded example of radiovangelism.

'In the beginning was the Rua,' Enoch goes on,

his voice thundering through the ballroom. 'And I'll wager that before there was even a name for history she rose as a mountain spring and swelled with every furlong as she spilled down our county's spine.'

A pause here, disturbed only by the solitary honk of a blown nose. Enoch can smell the sweat rising from his shirt.

'Now it is said that in the Rua's waters spawned the Salmon of Knowledge from which Fionn MacCumhaill took his wisdom. Was it not her fertile soil that seduced the Normans to build on these banks and people the river valley, and for the next eight hundred years gave you the gift of tillage and dairy farming? Indeed it was that soil.'

Someone shifts their chair with a scalp-crawling scrape. Enoch proceeds with his speech.

'In the winter of 1956 the Rua's waters froze solid enough for people to walk across, allowing men to pantomime the miracle of Our Lord upon the waves. But God be praised, the river thawed and flowed freely once again, carrying cots on her back and providing employment for so many townsmen freighting sand and goods downstream until the rail-way and new road stole her traffic.'

By now certain folk are looking at their watches and casting glances towards the door, and Enoch senses he's a hair's breadth from a slow handclap. He picks up the pace.

'She kept flowing throughout this very decade, bringing what meagre cheer she could when Murn seemed a forgotten place disowned by the rest of the country, when the sawmill's blades roared no more and then the granary and the maltings closed, their silos voided of grain, and publicans torched their premises for the insurance. No need to look so surprised now. Many of you know of what I speak.'

Another pause as Enoch probes the room with what he believes is a piercing gaze, but the intended moment of suspense is perforated by coughs and more chair-scraping. He scans his remaining script. Pages and pages left. Damn the schedule. Caffrey can play Ó'Riada to fill the space. He skips to the closing paragraphs.

'Yes, the Rua has served you without qualm or quarrel, she has fed you and watered you and asked for nothing in return. And so now I stand before you, still a newcomer to you kind people, but one who has been humbled by your welcome, and I commend that spirit of amity and fervently hope that I can continue to serve you here on Ballo Local Radio even half as nobly as that ever-faithful river Rua has served this town of Murn. As she was in the beginning, and will be in the end, forever and ever . . .'

Here he pauses once more, perhaps anticipating a response of 'Amen' or even a smattering of applause. Alas, there is nothing but dank silence, and over the radio waves, dead air. Enoch looks around the ballroom, his gaze returned by blank or nonplussed expressions, some of outright hostility, from expectant plebs denied their bread and circuses.

Andy Caffrey is gazing out the window. Enoch bends his head and quietly draws breath. These fine words have elicited nothing but a few baboon-faced yawns and surly expressions, and in his breast there beats a sad and nauseous heart. More long seconds of dead air as he takes a moment to recompose, then he lifts his head and says:

'Go in peace. Good night.'

Andy Caffrey snaps awake and cues the closing music, 'Mise Éire'. Enoch leaves the stage and hurries out the side door and positions himself in the hotel's lobby, pretending to read through the sheaves of his speech as the punters shuffle out. In his mind there still percolates hope that someone might stop and compliment his performance. But no, they disappear into the night, grumbling and mumbling and casting him dirty looks.

And now the spit is bitter in his mouth. He has

cast pearls before swine and they have turned up their piggy snouts. Scripture lends perspective but no solace: *Give not that which is holy unto the dogs, lest they trample your pearls under their feet, and turn again and rend you.* Now as he mounts the stairs and heads towards his room, a familiar sound insinuates itself into his ear. The ticking of a clock, the turning of a dial, a sequence of electromagnetic impulses translated into numbers, counting down the days until Lord knows what.

Fear not, dear Enoch, a voice tells him. One day your soul may flee the prison of this mortal coil and climb a golden burnished ladder on which the adders and asps can never find purchase or ascend. Your arrival may be heralded by an almighty trumpet blast and you will enter the savannah lands of Paradise, called home, my brother, at last called home, returned to eternity dressed in fine-spun gold and purple robes like Elvis Himself in Caesar's Palace, and a choir of golden angels will *Aaaaah* like a thousand Jordanaires and the King of Kings will enfold you in a warm embrace and kiss your cheek and whisper, 'Welcome, my son.'

The phone on his bedside table is ringing. When he answers it a woman asks for him by name and then identifies herself as Carmel Owens, ward nurse at Ballo General. She speaks for a moment and Enoch says, 'I see,' and again, 'I see,' then thanks the nurse and puts down the phone.

The room seems to pitch and spin as he searches for a not-so-dirty shirt and calls a taxi, and when it comes he hurries down the hall towards the stairs, pausing at the observatory tower to settle himself, and there he hears it again: the whirring of chopper blades, the *whomp* of herons' wings, distant gunfire, coming rains, and behind it all, his father's voice, his father's face, his father's ghost.

+ + + + + + + +

The following is taken from the transcript of the as yet unaired PBN radio series A Healer's Casebook: *interviews with Professor Charles Stafford, conducted by Bill Howard. Professor Stafford requested that certain comments be omitted from the prospective broadcast.*

Bill Howard: Professor, can you tell us what inspired Frank O'Reilly's theory of recurring flood patterns?

Charles Stafford: The short answer is his research. But he must have known what he was looking for. Most of the parish records and newspaper archives lodged in the original town library, built on the site now occupied by the Rua Hotel, were destroyed by water damage, so a lot of his evidence came from stray lines in almanacs and miscellanies, oral histories.

The historian Clementine Ryan gave him an anthology of folk songs including a lyric entitled 'The Devil's Elbow' which alluded to some mysterious

event that took place by the river Rua in the winter
of 1844. And there's a fairly well known court poem
called 'The River's Coming into Her Time' which
mentions a drowning cluster that occurred in 1760.
From scores, if not hundreds, of fragments, Frank
worked out a system.

Could you explain that system?
He believed the floods recurred at intervals of
twenty-eight, fifty-six and 112 years: 1956, 1844,
1788, 1760, 1648. All these floods caused drowning
clusters, the fatalities mostly male.

**Apparently Frank believed that certain rivers
obey a timer mechanism.**
That the river knows when to flood and freeze, yes.
He wrote: 'When placed in isolated laboratory en-
vironments, tubers, crustaceans, oysters, fish and insects retain the information of when to seed or flower
or reproduce. Controlled by their own endogenous
rhythms, even the humblest unicellular forms obey a
mysterious internal timer. They understand how to
interpret and decode complex magnetic, electrostatic
and electromagnetic signals from beyond their own
geophysical fields, and respond to this stimulus by
sprouting and spawning on schedule. In the cosmic

sense, all God's creatures know what time it is. So too
the river obeys an astral calendar.'

And not just in Murn.
No. According to data harvested by his Hearing Aid,
these 'flood-cull phenomena', as he called them, occurred all over the globe throughout the century:
Wales, the Isle of Wight, Nantucket, Newfoundland,
Micronesia and New Guinea. He was very excited
when a boy discovered an underground cave near
the entrance to the railway tunnel under Murn in the
spring of 1969.

Why?
On the walls were paintings depicting some nine
figures descending into the waters, captioned with
the words 'Man, death, water of life'. This suggested a
pattern that extended as far back as the Palaeolithic.

**Were these phenomena previously documented
and investigated?**
They might have been. As I said, flood damage destroyed most of the archives, so it's hard to tell.

**You've written about flood mythology going back
thousands of years. There's a recurring theme of**

mythological races of superhumans, the Nephilim and so on.

Most flood myths have this central motif. Hebrew scripture tells of a race of fallen angels who mated with human women and sired the Watchers. The Book of Genesis speaks of giants in the earth. Sumerian myths depict humanity as a mongrel race of slaves to the alien Annunaki who whenever there was a rebellion used floods to regain control. The god-like Archon grew jealous of men's attempts to scale the heavens and destroyed the Tower of Babel and sent a deluge to obliterate humankind. Irish folklore tells of the Tuatha Dé Danaan, the Fir Bolg, the Fomorians, the Elim, ancestral beings in league with nature, at war with man. Our Celtic Nephilim.

There's also a radical ecological element to all this. Echoes of Gaia's revenge.

The planet attempting to abort us. If she does not burn us off like bugs, or shake us off with tremors, she will drown us. Frank developed a theory that bodies of water generate signals which can be interpreted on a subconscious level by the human brain, as some believe music can transmit subliminal messages. He believed the river somehow sang out to the weak and ill as a kind of culling process.

I think some part of him believed mankind had become a degenerate species, dependent on technologies, cut off from our natural roots. And as more and more of us live in industrialised societies, we learn only from our own kind, and consequently our mental processes have become inbred, and our deeper, older instincts have atrophied. It was one of the reasons Frank eventually abandoned his Hearing Aid. He said it was just a toy. He came to believe that a machine will always lack the original potential of the human mind, with all its latent and untapped powers. I tend to think he was right. But then, the human brain is my bread and butter, so to speak. My personal feeling is that since the invention of the H-bomb, mankind has suffered concurrent periods of mass mania and depression. We've been made sick by the knowledge that our species is capable of destroying itself.

Something happened in the summer of 1969 that changed the course of Frank O'Reilly's life and work.

That's right. This must remain off the record, but I'll tell you for context. That summer Frank's son Enoch stole into his workshop and tampered with the Hearing Aid's settings. No damage was done, but Frank

was troubled by the notion that he had somehow corrupted his son, exposed him to things he shouldn't
have seen or heard at that age, so he told the boy it no
longer worked. He frequently expressed regret that he
hadn't made the basement more secure. He locked the
Hearing Aid in his cellar and from then he worked in
a cabin he'd built in the Mweelrooney woods for field-
work. It was there he began to investigate more . . .
esoteric methods, I suppose you'd say.

Such as?
An arcane form of water divining. He cut himself a
hazel wand.

Why?
He believed it would act as a sort of conducting aerial, allow him to interpret the sounds of the streams
and tributaries. When he returned to his cabin, he
transcribed what he thought he'd heard.

**There was a case of an illiterate man from the
Southern states of America who believed he could
channel the Holy Spirit by transcribing running
water patterns.**
That was Frank's territory. He was also interested in
tribal shamans achieving altered states through long-

breath vocal emanations. He believed that if he generated a sort of infrasonic hum from the diaphragm, he could effectively block the buzz and chatter of his conscious mind and allow the subconscious – the second mind – to operate unimpeded. He practised lulling himself into a state of optimum receptivity.

Meditation in other words.
A fairly advanced form of it. Perhaps you've heard of Pythagoras's conception of the universe as a sphere in which celestial bodies turn in concentric patterns, fixed to a great wheel, giving us our diurnal cycle of day and night, then giving us in turn seasons and centuries. The Greeks believed the movement of sun, moon and planets produced a sound, the hum of each cosmic body tuned to a different pitch commensurate with the ratio of their orbits, much as the sound produced by a string adheres to its length and tension. The universe's symphony, its movement, is played by a gigantic musical instrument, a lyre – hence the universal monochord. Frank believed if he could produce a microcosm of that sound from within his own body, the mysteries of the universe might reveal themselves to him.

You were sceptical?

I was perturbed. You have to understand, Frank was a rationalist. Yet here he was behaving like a nineteenth-century medium. Night after night he chanted the same trigger words he had programmed into the Hearing Aid: 'river', 'flood', 'drowning' and so on. And he kept records. Throughout June, July and August of 1969 he filled dozens of notebooks.

What did they contain?

Automatic writing. He said some nights it was as if an invisible hand was moving his pen across the page, and he had no knowledge of the content until he emerged from his trance and read what he – if indeed it was 'he' – had written. When he reviewed these 'mediated' writings, he isolated the most relevant entries.

Would you care to read some of them?

Certainly.

AD 1399: *Loch Lerne turned to blood. Gouts as the lights of animals littered the shore.*

AD 1101. *Excessive rains and flood. Loughs, pools and rivers turned solid with ice, which were as roads for cattle.*

AD 804. *Floods of rain in Lagenia, causing streams to swell. Many signs and wonders. A dragon sighted upon the moon. Ships with their crews seen in the air.*

AD 660. Spontaneous floods, brought about by pray-
ers of saints and abbots, as the population was so
great a scarcity of provisions and insufficiency of soil
threatened.

AD 443. A hairy star appeared in the southern sky.
The river rose and breached its banks, but there had
fallen not a drop of rain.

They sound almost like archaic journal entries.
Indeed.

Do you think they're authentic?
I can't say. Frank believed he had channelled them
from the collective unconscious, race memory,
whatever you want to call it.

How was his mental state?
Erratic. He had all but abandoned his wife and son.
On the nights we still met for a drink he seemed dis-
tracted, agitated. He told me that when he tried to
sleep he heard the river babble inside his mind. She
was the only reality – 'riverality' as he called it. He
ate, slept, breathed and dreamed the river, wrote and
thought in 'riverish', sat up all night transcribing the
sounds he heard.

Did you see any of these transcriptions?

They looked like soundwave patterns. I couldn't imagine how they would be deciphered. But Frank was convinced the Rua was trying to communicate something. He said that if a man could channel ancestral voices, why not the sounds of nature, the river herself? Our bodies are mostly water. From water we come.

What was your response?

To ask him to come into St Edmund's. He wouldn't hear of it.

When did you see him last?

Late August 1969. He was hypomaniacal, I would say. He believed the river's signal was being corrupted by its passage through the air. He was working on ways to immerse himself in water long enough to decipher it. He kept talking about Pushkaram, the rite of river worship that occurs every dozen years in India when the *rishis* enter the water for a sacred swim in the company of gods. And he had some sort of fixation with the story of the Salmon of Knowledge. I must admit, I was rather upset when he left that night.

You never saw him again.
No. Frank was officially a missing person, but Kath
leen managed to have him declared legally deceased.
Something to do with the insurance money, I imagine. Obviously you can't broadcast that.

[Ends]

+ + + + + + + +

The Womb & the Grave

October 1984

The autumn evening sky is whey-faced and grey and an early autumn breeze patterns the river that parallels the road out of Murn. What light there is barely penetrates Enoch O'Reilly's tinted glasses, and he does not hear a word the driver says as the taxi bears them both towards Ballo General Hospital.

Kathleen collapsed on the ferry home from Fishguard. According to the nurse she was listed by her maiden name, Devereux, on the manifest and it took until now to find a number and contact her next of kin. I'm sorry, said the nurse, but your mother's suffered a massive stroke.

Enoch pays the driver and hurries up the steps of Ballo General and makes inquiries at the desk and is directed to room 12, Ward B on the Hyacinth Wing. The corridor seems to lurch and roll as he propels himself into the ward's unrelenting whiteness.

At first he cannot distinguish his mother from the

other withered souls sunk into their beds. Her face is slack all down one side and there are tubes taped to her nose and mouth. How bad, he asks the nurse, and the nurse says very bad. That morning Kathleen brought up coffee grounds – half digested blood – and Father Callaghan administered the sacraments.

Enoch takes a seat and grasps his mother's scrawny claw in his own big hand and there's nothing for it but to wait it seems, wait and watch, and crave a drink, and wait again.

After several hours have passed he rises from his chair to walk fluorescent-lit halls in the stuffy heat and small hours' silence. Before long he happens upon the hospital's little chapel and takes a pew and gazes upon the soft light of the altar. As he's slumped there in the silence, transfixed by the gentle glimmering of candles, Enoch's eyes droop to half-lidded and soon they close completely. *The earth has bubbles*, says his mother's voice. *You can feel it in your stones.* A hand travels between his legs and cups his sac and gives a bit of a heft, and the sensation is so real it startles him awake. He raises his eyes to see Nurse Owens framed in the doorway by the font, backlit by a halo of fluorescent light.

'Peripheral pulse is gone,' she says. 'Best come with me.'

Enoch follows her down the corridor, and even as he enters the ward he can feel a change in the atmosphere, as though the event of Kathleen's dying has permeated the entire wing. He asks the nurse if he can have a moment alone with his mother and she says of course and pulls the curtains around the bed.

Kathleen's eyelids flutter but she does not wake. The clock mounted above the bed tolls the moments in time with Enoch's own pulse and his mother's slow and laboured breath. Every so often he glances at the progress of its hands as if there's some preordained schedule to which this ordeal must adhere, and his breathing merges with Kathleen's and he waits and waits it out until, sometime in the depths of night, he is roused from his chair by a scurry of nurses around the bed. Kathleen has begun to slip. Enoch takes her hand and monitors her rhythms' ebb.

Now in his mind they walk together, him and his mum, descending into an underworld trembling with throes and moans, and when at last they reach the place where they must part he squeezes her tiny claw and turns back to the light, leaving Kathleen to the darkness. When she reaches her dying place she inhales a final gasp of air and then gives up the ghost in a long and awful exhalation, and in this instant Enoch finds himself seeing two portals to eternity, the womb and the grave, one door closed as another opens, as voices coax him home.

And now in his loneliness and despair he cries out to the only spirit he has known as kindred, but there is no response. He cannot picture Elvis's face nor hear his voice because Elvis has forsaken him, nothing remains only the bones of his mother and the ghost of his father and the sound of the river and the *whomp* of wings and now Enoch knows the despair of the priest who has lost his faith, the body that has given up the ghost, that long last voiding of the essence. For a world without a mother or a father or a King is a cold and desolate place, and nothing remains but fragments, echoes, the sound of that old Holy Ghost Radio babbling in the river air.

+ +

Like the druid Finegas I have fished for the Salmon of Knowledge, not

+ +

he RIVER knows what time it is.

+ +

RE 13 DAYS TO THE FLOOD

+ +

+ + + + + + + +

VI

THE BROTHERHOOD OF THE FLOOD

+ + + + + + + +

The Last Temptation of Alice Stafford

1975–1984

The babble became unbearable somewhere in the middle of Alice Stafford's final college year. She couldn't tune it out. Certain nights the ceiling looked like an astral map composed of numerals and decimal points or Morse dots, and her fingers gripped the sides of her bed as she experienced beatitudes so profound they were traumatic, and the perfect connectedness of everything caused her frontal lobe to hum, and even while she slept her mind seemed to radiate pure heat.

Alice Stafford was brought up well. Her mother kept a clean house and a beautiful garden and her father was an educated man, but even the Professor wouldn't have believed her conduct throughout that month. She spent and swore like a sailor and slept with anything in a skirt and raved and raged until her mind had fairly boiled itself to steam. Then came the intermittent spells, up and down, alternating currents. She was restless and she was peevish and sometimes the urge to get twisted on whiskey was almost carnal so get twisted she did, and if anyone asked about her studies she said she might as well put her brain inside a glass case and throw peas at it.

One day she woke in her underwear, terrified, her body covered with briar welts, her toenails and the soles of her feet caked with dirt. A bottle of Smirnoff and a fistful of Seconals and she dialled 999 and said this is not an SOS but could you tell me how many of these things a girl can take with alcohol. The switchboard operator said stay on the line and keep talking.

The ambulance rushed Alice to A&E where they pumped her stomach and kept her in for observation. Her first thought was for her dad, her great strong oak. When he heard what she had done he took it as well as any father could and insisted she must get well no matter what. He recommended she sign herself in for three months minimum and she stood weeping in his arms.

St Edmund's was a private institution. Gone were all vestiges of grim Victoriana, of Bedlam and Broadmoor horrors, electrodes and clamps and restraints. The place was run like a strict hotel, meals and meds and changes of bedding and rise and shine at 6 a.m. Rooms resounded with radio chatter and TV laugh-tracks, the clank of radiators. Wisps of the female patients' fragrances pervaded the halls. From the great bay windows you could see the low limestone cliffs that frowned upon sand-spits clamped across the Ruan estuary mouth. The nearby sea was a constant sighing presence and there was an expansiveness outside, a sense of infinite space and sky that seemed to mock those confined to the hospital's crooked walls and see-saw floors.

Alice's counsellor told her she must train her mind to be still and calm. She must learn to control the babble, he said. Alice promised to do her best, but by Christ it was a hard old autumn. Mornings were the worst, when she felt so feeble she could barely speak, all her hours dissolving into one long crying jag, curled on her bed keening and cradling herself like a thing made of griefs, guttural weeping like that of a widow or a sickly pup.

She went about her days befuddled, drained of blood. She sat like a catatonic in the dayroom and watched children's television shows and lit one cigarette off the last and swore she'd quit and made as if to break the whole bunched bouquet of cigarettes in half. She was plagued with morbid thoughts, could feel her soul eroding cell by cell, a terrible darkness governing all.

She made a pact with herself that if the pain did not end of its own accord she would find a way to end it, do it and do it quick, a belt looped over a shower rail or a bleed-out in a hot bath or a single leap out a high window. She made secret deadlines in her diary and there was comfort in this knowing that the horror was not indefinite, it was simply a matter of will, of screwing her nerve to the sticking point.

Then the darkness began to lift. It was slow at first, inexorable. The pills were trial and error and therapy wore her out, but she got out of bed and took one breath at a time and cell by cell the dread receded and her moods improved and she mentioned finding work. She persuaded her father to arrange an internship for her at an accountant's office in Ballo town.

From then on she spent her days in a tangle of telephones, one eye trained on the IBM screen that channelled the Ceefax feed linked to the Dow Jones. She could stay in that boxy little office until night, spectacles balanced on her nose as she lost herself in the coils of some discrepancy between expenses declared and receipts provided. She cut her auburn bob into a brutal number two and laid off the make-up and shed her jewellery and wore conservative suits, determined to conform not with the office girls with their perms and pastels but with the no-frills males. She had lunch with her father every Friday and fussed about how gaunt he looked, his hair now thin and white, but he just smiled and squeezed her hand and changed the subject back to work or the weather or anything but himself.

Sometimes she raided her savings and splurged on weekend R&R trips to Paris or Barcelona and wandered down the Champs-Elysées or the Ramblas alone, wishing all the time she had someone to share it with, someone to hold her hand as she made her tipsy pilgrimage through silent snow to stand outside Hansa by the Wall in Berlin where her beloved Bowie had bellowed 'Heroes' into microphones placed at intervals of one to forty paces.

She felt alone, really felt it now, in her bones, the way the elderly feel the cold. She sat sad and solitary in *Bierkellers* and singles bars waiting for The One. She stared at herself in mirrors and saw a willowy girl desperate to be touched, and she knew those she desired could smell that needy pheromone and so avoided her. Sometimes she was so tightly wound she spasmed when strangers brushed against her.

She had a few blind encounters but when the fun and the drink wore off she lay in her bed hungover and guilty and sour. She ached when she saw sweethearts walk the boulevards outside arm in arm.

She craved a warm body to hold onto in the night, someone to rub her shoulders or make her a cup of tea in the morning, someone to plain and simply love.

An ad-hoc shopping trip to Amsterdam nose-dived into a lost weekend and then a full-on kami-kaze mission. After three or four doubles in a trashy disco-bar she met a twenty-year-old stunner in a bustier named Mai-Li and was so desperate to kiss and hold her she put a hundred quid's worth of guilders on the counter and told this complete and total stranger it was hers if she'd spend the weekend in her hotel room, nothing sleazy, they'd just watch television and order room service and lie in one another's arms.

The girl said yes and they toasted the transaction. Blitzed beyond all reckoning, they stumbled to her room. Mai-Li padded inside like a wary cat, wasn't satisfied until she'd lit a candle and draped her scarf over the lampshade and made it look like a sacred place, a shrine.

They woke late in a tangle of limbs and walked the canal the following afternoon. Something about the girl's eyes, the way the skin beneath looked bruised, the way her face was so taut it seemed the flesh had melted away leaving only bone, made Alice reach for her hand as the waters whispered. A breeze rippled across their surface and a feeling came upon her like when you swim too far out and it's getting dark.

By the Sunday morning Mai-Li was gone. Alice lay on the bed and wept. Then she went downstairs to the hotel bar where she drank until the sadness faded to a throb.

That night she went in search of a place she'd heard about from a business client, a private club. She was shown into a sort of anteroom with paper changing screens and a bead-veiled partition and a burgundy kimono draped across a chair. She undressed and put on the kimono and sipped a drink and when she was ready she went on through the beads. Beyond a heavy curtain was total black. She felt thin bamboo mats underfoot, smelled wisps of perfume, sensed movement, respiration. Something touched her arm and then the tie string was undone and the kimono slid from her shoulders. Lips brushed her ears and neck and breasts, the soft clicking sounds of kisses, and heat spread downwards through her body in a slow and lovely detonation. Someone kissed her stomach and then her hip and she sort of buckled or collapsed upon the bamboo mat and parted her legs and allowed herself to feel it all, all of it, and she moaned like some profane prayer oh fuck oh fuck, and when it was done fingers caressed her face and brow and seemed to say there now, soft voices whispering, and it was sublime, this slipping unto death after the throes, slipping into oblivion, and she felt almost cured or pardoned, absolved of some unnameable sin.

That night when Alice called home her father's voice was a Valium monotone. Her mother's test results were worse than bad, inoperable. And all Alice could think was what a strange word that is, inoperable.

Her mother took a year to die. The bearing witness to it was a kind of death in life and the Professor took it hard. He cancelled all public engagements. Alice assumed her mother's role as his counsellor and foil and persuaded him to accept an autumn-semester lecturing post in the States.

With her father gone she walked for miles in the evenings along the riverside where everything smelled ripe and damp and on the point of rot. One night her steps led her where they always did, the mooring pylon, the woodenworks at Ballo Harbour. There she stood upon the dock and it seemed she was fated to always return to here, her path preordained, and she decided the shape of life is circular, an inoperable loop. No matter what turn she took it would always lead back to this.

Lights glimmered around the harbour. She gazed into the gloom and saw drifting towards the swollen estuary mouth a fallen tree. She imagined descending the steps of the jetty and wading into the water to put her arms around its trunk, allowing the current to take her.

And as the estuary waters lulled her near Alice at last let go of everything, the fallen tree, her past, her pain, her name. Her eyes filled with water as an old song came into her mind, and she heard herself sing of summer kisses, winter tears and she whispered come home daddy, hurry home.

+ + + + + + + +

The Story of Isaac

God's truth I wished you dead so I could bury you and mourn you out of me and suffer no more. No more would I wake afeared that if I didn't get you back you'd find another man's bed to warm. Nor would I moan in my sleep dreaming your voice or the taste when I pushed my tongue into your mouth to purge you of other men so all you would have known was me, and this knowing would silence the shadows that jeered me in the night and said I couldn't compare with the ones that came before.

I stayed in bed for days thinking about you and me and the day we met, on the bus to the Bob Dylan concert at Slane. I stared at you all the way and when the bus let us off at the site we started talking. The light was very strange that day you couldn't credit it the sun looked sort of bloodshot, muggy weather, close, everything slow and still and there were thunder showers and when the sun came out steam rose off the road in a mist that came to your waist.

I took your hand as we followed the crowd and stepped over bodies and picnic baskets and there were gasps and wows at the sight of all those people gathered on the valley's slope. The crowd swelled all the way up the hill as the sun went down and it was like everyone in the world was waiting for Bob Dylan to come on stage and you wondered what it must feel like to be the only name on so many people's tongues.

A ripple went through the field and you squeezed my hand and your face was like a lassie's at the circus. You'd seen him through a gap in the barriers. He was walking from the backstage cabins towards a ramp and as he approached the stage he seemed to change or take the shape of other forms, a soldier or a priest. He wore a long coat and carried his guitar over his shoulder and his face was covered in make-up and his eyes were black and the band were up there playing the first song, I think it was the one about Highway 61.

Then he put his harmonica in the harness and strummed his guitar and sang it's a hard rain's a-gonna fall and the hill lit up with thousands of lights, sure it looked almost lantern-lit and the dew shone in the twilight and I pulled you near to me and everything faded but the song and we had neither want nor care and I felt the memory become a memory then, and if only we could've stayed that way forever but sure we couldn't and then the show was over.

Fireworks ripped and burst as we climbed the hill and all the people looked like tribes from olden times returning from some kind of battle or harvest-bringing or whatever. It was dark when we got to the coach. I remember the sound of the big diesel engine rumbling and the blue striplights on the ceiling and when we took our seats you put your head on my shoulder and slept near all the way to Murn.

The driver stopped at the crossroads and I wrote my number on the back of the concert ticket and put it in your pocket and kissed your cheek and I didn't look back until my feet were on the road. You blew me a kiss through the window and I set off home across the river field and then the beet field and the meadow. The dawn was ripening as I crossed and the red sun rose and it seemed like everything in the world that day was glad to see what was in my heart and reflected it in kind and I was happy sure I did not know what was to come.

Your family said I was too grown-up for you but I allowed in some countries a man will take a bride of twelve. Maybe they thought I was not good enough and maybe they were right but we had some sport at times. We used to drive the back roads with the windows down and your hair blowing and me talking on the CB radio and the way you laid your hand over mine on the gearstick made my heart beat like the clappers. I put an old mattress in the back for us to lie down on but you would not lie down with me yet.

Then the big day came when you turned eighteen and you arrived on my doorstep unannounced and no sooner across the threshold than you took my hand and led me to the bed. You were a woman then and like a woman you had learned to speak your mind. You did not like that farmhouse, not one bit, the cold and the damp and the dirt. I said feel free to make it fit for her ladyship's habitation and you said you wouldn't be no man's skivvy. It was like you showed me one side of yourself when we were courting and another when the courting was done. I couldn't stir out the door without twenty questions, where was I bound, what time would I be back. Many's the night I spent in the Spoke telling my troubles to Billy Litt and he said it's like the fine-looking bird in the circus who makes lions jump through burning hoops, if a woman can do that to a lion think what she can do to a man.

Some nights after closing time I would park at Heavendale and listen to the talk on the CB radio and for no good reason I felt very vexed at everything around me, the river gossiping and the wind moaning like an old person and the mountains stood too close together and the sky that looked like a rug on a washing line, and I cursed this awful place where nothing would ever happen that hadn't happened a hundred times before.

Then you got it into your head that I'd done the dirt on you I never did but still you let fly at me. I stuck my hands in my pockets to keep from striking you back but then something happened and you were on the floor with a bloody lip. I went to put my arm around you but you bet me away and then rang your brother to come and collect you. When he arrived I went out to make you see reason but he barred the way and it nearly came to blows. That brother of yours was a scourge.

Well after you left I was in an awful state. I was afeared I'd never see your face nor hold your hand again I lost my reason entirely I seen you like a ghost in every aspect and the only thing that would ease my pain was drink. My mind was full of pictures of you with other men. I thought about the river at the bottom of the river field and the sound of it got in on me sure it was the last thing I heard before I fell asleep and first thing when I woke.

Autumn brought such a cold as I have never felt and one morning when I rose to bring in the herd I was very weak and the light of day looked too bright and I knew this could not go on. I swore I would cry no more I would cut you out of my mind. I took a notion then and got the old guitar out of the spare room and fooled with it and as long as my fingers found the chords I would not think of you. The big thick strings bit into my fingers and reminded me I was alive but sure as soon as I put the guitar away the fear returned.

One night I was in the Spoke and a fiddle was passed around but no one would play until an old man took it in his hands. Then a couple got up to dance and I watched how they held each other sort of formal the way all old people dance, and my heart felt scraped or raw or maybe I was only jarred. There was nothing gentle in the way the man drew the bow or pressed the strings as though to hurt the wood. I went home and tried to get the same sounds from the old guitar but I could not and it vexed me rightly so I got the hatchet and splintered it to kindling.

You said always I expected the worst and in so expecting summoned it, well there might be something in that. All I know for a cert is what happened last week in the Spoke when I was drinking with Billy Litt and he said he saw you at the station and that you weren't alone. Who were you with I said. Young Owen Cody, he told me and that you were headed west. Where west I said to Billy. Drumgloan he said to me.

Well I came up in a rise of sweat and the drink soured in my guts, what Billy Litt said had pure straightened me out. I put my coat on and he said where are you going with your arse in two halves and no sign of it healing and I told him I was going to bring you home and he had a right laugh at that. To Hell or to Connacht, he said.

I went on up to the farm and got the gun and put it in my gear bag and I rang Davey, I woke him up and said you may look in on the herd in the morning and half asleep he said he would.

I drove right through the night, talking to myself on the CB radio just like this. The sound of my own voice kept me awake sure I thought I was on some big highway and could go for days without running out of road. I kept my eyes on the white line and the rearview mirror watching for the squadder for my tax disc was out and one of the back lights was on the blink. I thought of you and Owen Cody all the way.

I kept looking at the shotgun beside me on the seat and wondering whether or not I'd have the stones to use it come the time.

The sun rose up and I crossed into Connacht and stopped at a Shell station and filled the tank. People say that part of the world is beautiful but it's ugly as sin sure O'Connor's Pass is only barren and scabby, rocks and craters and waterlogged hollows, big pissholes, a mean little road snaking up the rise of it, and the landscape stretching off would make your stomach turn with the thought of falling, and God's truth I saw the Devil's face carved there in the mountainside.

The car's engine started to chuck and then cut out but I got her over the summit and let her roll down-mountain and when the land levelled out I pushed her off the road into a paddock and locked the doors. I took the gear bag with the shotgun in it and set off on foot. By now it was full morning.

Drumgloan was only a village with souvenir shops and tables outside tea shops and pastry shops and nice little places like that. I walked the main street north and south and haunted that town all morning and still no sign of you nor Owen Cody. I rang Davey and Davey said I may come home he wouldn't be responsible for these animals no more. I told Davey what Billy Litt said and that I had to bring you back and he said Billy Litt was a black liar and any clown would know full well he'd sent me on a wild goose chase and when would I ever learn.

Well now I was fully straightened out I felt some fool I can tell you. Billy Litt had wound me up for sport. I went down to the beach and rolled a smoke. A man and a woman stood together on the shore. The man said something to the woman and they moved away on down the strand and I wanted to tell them I wasn't about to harm no one but they were already too far gone so I sat for a bit and smoked and listened to the waves and the sea looked very vexed.

It cost me dear to get the van towed off the mountain but when she was fixed I drove her home and soon as I got in the door I went upstairs and took to the bed. Davey called round and said get up out of that. I said that I would not. Davey started in on me again, he said if I didn't do something about them animals he was going to report me. I said Davey get away from me. I knew he was right but still.

There were forty head of cattle in that field. I took the gun and two boxes of shells from the cupboard and I went out with the dog and rounded the herd and shot every beast among them. The dog took off in fright but he soon came back and I did for him as

well. The river will take them soon enough I think.
It's rising by the new time and sure I'll be waiting
when it comes.

+ +

OMING INTO HER TIME.

+ +

hy

+ +

RE 10 DAYS TO THE FLOOD

+ +

+ + + + + + + +

VIII

ENOCH O'REILLY AND THE COMING
OF THE FLOOD

+ + + + + + + +

Shall We Gather at the River

Late October 1984

Ballo Local Radio announces Kathleen O'Reilly's memorial in the Rua Hotel ballroom at eight o'clock on the night of October twenty-third. All are invited to gather and share griefs and remembrances of the deceased, light refreshments provided.

The appointed hour arrives. Grey stacking chairs semicircle a dining table on which the hotel's caterers have placed a tea urn, a tower of styrofoam cups and a platter heaped with wafer biscuits. Maroon drapes are drawn across floor-to-ceiling windows but the air in here is perishing.

Enoch reaches into his pocket and sneaks a nip of brandy from the hip flask tucked in his frock coat, small protection against the autumn chill, and his lips move slightly as he formulates an opening few words in memory of his mum. He envisions townspeople paying their respects and grasping his hand, transfusing strength, nodding in sympathy and making sounds of comfort and reassurance.

By nine o'clock the hip flask is half empty. Not a single soul has come. Not a friend or relation of Kathleen's, not even a single freeloader or a cadge, and Enoch wonders if he is such a pariah among men, if his existence is so odious to the people of this town that it taints even the memory of his recently departed mother.

Bitterly he packs away his things and buttons up his coat and hurries out the hotel's front doors. A cold wind whistles off the river. On he forges up the prom towards the bridge that arches across the Rua's highway and there he stops to take a pull of brandy. He gazes over the edge and, deciding some sort of gesture is required, uncaps the hip flask and tips it and as the wind disperses the thin stream of liquid into a hundred pearls that fall towards the water, he summons from his lungs a manly baritone:

'*Shall we gather at the river . . .*'

Then he feels all goodness draining from his soul. Only a year ago it felt as though the Holy Ghost danced upon his tongue, but now it's gone. Perhaps Kathleen was right. A great man cannot be beholden to his fellow man. A great man must forsake his earthly gods and put childish things away. We labour at the hem of our King and then we butcher him.

This is the way of the world: all mythologies are Oedipal at their core. We murder the father to steal his fire, and we are murdered in turn. And what of the mother, then? She is gone. Her son will soon return to Mweelrooney, called home, at last, called home.

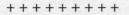

The Lost Alice

Late October 1984

You could see Charles Stafford walk the country roads throughout that month, and when his eyes began to burn with light you knew he must have glimpsed her in the thickets and the groves, his vanished child returned at last to ease his suffering. She flitted like a chimera across his field of vision, skirting between the moon's glittering beams, a faerie queen or changeling or a creature made of mist, and he hurried after her image murmuring her name.

Alice had disappeared the month before and no one could tell him what had become of her, and that not-knowing was the torture, the vicious mystery of her disappearance, a question that could not be answered giving unto the obsession of the bereft, a horrible thought flitting through the woodlands of his mind that every passing day he did not hear from her the more likely it was the water had called her home and there would be no resolution nor end to grieving unless – until – the river returned her body to his arms.

And so you'd see him in the townlands, a fisherman's slicker around his bony shoulders, white hair sticking out from beneath a woollen cap. Folk would remark how anguished-looking he'd become, for faith you should have known him in his prime: a proper gent with cufflinks and a paisley tie in a perfect Windsor knot. Now look at him wandering the town, his name well known among the drinkers and the betting men: the fallen Prof., the poor misfortunate. They awaited his knock on the doors of snugs and glanced up from their papers when they heard his voice, asking for his Alice. In every pub in Murn or Ballo Town, always the same inquiry. And the drinkers would call for him to come and sit, you're letting out the heat.

He might be seen later by the riverside, talking to the fishermen in their oilskins and their waders, or wandering the woodenworks on the quay, or grabbing the arms of bettors at the dog track, pushing a photograph into their hands. He would describe for them his daughter's emerald eyes and pale white skin, her elegant fingers and auburn hair. He had become a local curiosity, a character, the educated man who roamed the land half-mad with worry for his girl.

Some said he was seen as far afield as Carlow and Kilkenny. Motorists slowed to offer him a lift or to inquire if he was lost. Sometimes strays or mongrel dogs accompanied him on his wanderings, padding ahead like a scruffy motorcade. Crows and ravens circled about his head reporting tidings from afar, and it seemed even the wild things of the gripe were his trusted confidants. Still he tramped the roads, pausing only when his strength gave out, and at such times the sight he made was very sorrowful, slumped under a tree like some weary poet contemplating heaven above and the worms beneath.

And any soul who came close enough might have heard him utter *Alice*, as though to speak her name repeatedly might invoke her form, until the word itself detached from all memory and meaning and became another thing entirely, a mantra, an incantation, and he'd continue muttering it until the light dimmed on the fields and the jackdaws' chatter hushed and a merciful darkness descended on the land.

He kept on with his quest. When unsure of how to proceed he'd consult the moon and follow where it counselled. His face was skull-shaped now and his body emaciated, returned to the state of his urchinhood, those grimy childhood mornings in Dublin's inner city when he'd had to fight for scraps.

Then one night by the river's edge he glimpsed a host of shimmering lights at play, like fireflies or river wisps or gossamer. Under the moon that was once a mother looking down upon the Liberties, and who still looked down on Murn, he saw her there, his stolen child suspended, frozen in a twilight realm, beckoning, beckoning.

+ + + + + + + +

The Last Revival Hour

Late October 1984

Good evening. This is Ballo Local Radio News at nine.

Detectives at Murn garda station have concluded that the fire that ravaged the New Larkin Park council estate outside Murn last month was malicious in origin. The blaze, which began in the early hours of September first, gutted more than half of the thirty-four properties, causing hundreds of thousands of pounds' worth of damage. Sergeant Matthew Davin told Ballo Local Radio that evidence discovered at the scene indicated the perpetrator used oil siphoned from the heating tanks behind each residence to start the blaze.Construction work on the estate, a joint venture between private developers and Ballo Council, was completed last August. The fire occurred a week before the first residents were due to move in. Gardaí say investigations are ongoing. Repair and rebuilding is due to begin again in the new year.

Today in the District Court Mr David Miller, a

forty-year-old farmer from Donaldstown, Murn, sued for compensation from Mr Mossy Dempsey, Blackbridge, over the purchase of a breeding bullock. The complainant testified that a local vet informed him the bullock had only one descended testicle. Mr Dempsey's counsel contended that such a defect need not affect the animal's husbandry. He added that his client believed Mr Miller had badly neglected the animal, and on examination discovered evidence of tearing in the bullock's rectal wall. Under questioning, the complainant admitted that the other bullocks in the herd had been mounting the animal in question. 'Even they could tell he wasn't a proper bull,' he said. The case continues tomorrow.

Spokesmen for the Waxon Factory in Murn have announced today that there will be another round of job losses this month. Up to a dozen men at the textiles and manufacturing plant are due to be laid off before December, the second spate of redundancies this year. Reports of the lay-offs come amidst speculation that the Waxon company is about to close all Irish operations. Union representatives were vehement in their denunciation of the enforced redundancies.

In other news, holidaymakers and visitors to Mweelrooney beach witnessed a rare sight this week, as a minke whale was washed up on shore. The twenty-

foot mammal was first spotted on Friday morning by a passer-by. Volunteers from the Irish Seal Sanctuary attended to the corpse, taking a sample. The whale will be buried today, in situ on the beach, by Ballo County Council.

Now to sport, and the Murn Satellites under-twenty-one football team suffered a humiliating defeat at the hands of Ballo Rangers in the county semi-final at Somers Park last night. The game began badly for the Satellites when star player Owen Cody was sent off twenty minutes into the first half for striking the Rangers' full back. The home team were subsequently defeated by a fifteen-point margin in what manager Tommy Lennon described as their poorest performance for many years.

Tomorrow's weather, and the Met Office has forecast temperatures of six to eight degrees Celsius, cloudy and overcast in the morning, with rains expected towards the end of the week.

That's all from the Ballo Local news desk. Our next update is at ten.

+ + + + + + + +

October twenty-sixth, and the strangest of all *Revival Hour* shows is broadcast. There is no audience in the Rua Hotel ballroom, but Enoch O'Reilly instructs Andy Caffrey that no matter what transpires he must keep that red light lit. When the news desk's signature music bombasts itself to silence Andy cues a minute of 'Blue Moon' and then the fade, then Enoch speaks:

'You are listening to *O'Reilly's Revival Hour Live*,' he says. 'Tonight's broadcast is in memory of Kathleen O'Reilly.'

A pause.

'Little children, keep yourselves from idols.'

That's all. Six words from John's gospel, followed by fifty-three minutes of silence.

All across the town, Ballo Local listeners are puzzled by the void of sound. At the hotel's reception desk the phone rings and goes unanswered, but in the ballroom all is as still and peaceful as a tomb.

+ + + + + + + +

Enoch O'Reilly Goes Home

31 October, the day before the Flood

Twenty miles south of Murn, just beyond the village of Mweelrooney, Ballo Manor looks desolate. A sign on the gate warns against trespassers. A stony lane crawls a hundred-odd yards towards a brambled yard. Crows loiter on the overhead wires like hoodlums. Seagulls strafe the fields.

Enoch pays the taxi driver and hauls his suitcase from the boot and fumbles for the keys given to him by his late mother's solicitor. This house in which he was born, the house to which he returns, is in a state of bad neglect. But Kathleen never considered selling the property, the solicitor said. It was to be her only son's inheritance.

A bit of key-jiggling and the door unlocks. Post litters the front hall, mostly bills. Enoch goes through to the parlour. The walls give off the chill of too many nights without a fire. His shoulders are tense and tight. He moves from room to room opening windows, stepping over the cellar trapdoor like a man might avoid a grave. High up on pegs there rests his father's shotgun.

The telephone is situated on the antique table in the hall, beside it the phone directory and a stack of yellowed *Woman's Ways*, kept for the patterns. Enoch picks up the phone and the dial tone clicks and hums. For a moment he considers calling the operator and asking to speak to his mum. For some reason he's picturing seabirds flying inland, livestock drawing close to town.

He tips Scotch into a china teacup and builds a fire in the parlour fireplace but the wood is damp and soon goes out. For want of more to do he takes down his father's shotgun from its pegs and cleans it with a shine-rag, and when he has drunk enough to warm his gut his troubled bones groan enough's enough, so he takes the shotgun by the forestock and the bottle by the neck and the teacup between his teeth and mounts the stairs to his parents' bedroom. There he props the shotgun against the wall and lies fully clothed on the old brass bed amidst mildew smells and cold and clammy sheets. Birds flutter in the chimney flue and coat hangers and shoes seem to scuttle about in his mother's wardrobe. His long frock coat is hung upon the door like a great satanic bat.

Now sleep comes upon Enoch like a sickness. He dreams in washed-out monochrome and copper-stained sepia. He is lost in a forest and wants to cry for help but his lips are stitched shut. He is trapped in his father's cellar and the Holy Ghost Radio issues static and this is how the night goes, squirming and turning until he is awoken by the sound of hammering on the rooftop and the windows and in the gutters, increasing, intensifying, a commonplace sound that strikes unaccountable dread in his human heart, but when his eyes snap open it stops – never was – and he lies there quietly, as though the slightest movement might cause his bed to pitch. He rises from the bed and pours another drink. Then he takes the shotgun into the crook of his arm and descends the stairs and that's when he sees it, the faintest chink of light.

The cellar trapdoor is swollen from damp and raised off its jamb. Enoch puts down his drink and raises the gun. The padlock shatters under the repeated blows of the shotgun's stock. The hatch opens with a moan and the waft of decades pollutes the house, a musty, pungent smell like wet clothes left too long in the drum. The cellar is bathed in pale light.

He descends the steps, and slowly he goes, for he does not trust those boards. And now he sees the silhouette of Frank's machine, that great black box transmitter draped in a thin white sheet, and a slow tide of nausea rises in his blood as he realises his father lied. The machine was down here all these years, functioning perfectly and waiting for his return. Light gleams from beneath the caul, goes dark, gleams again. The fine hairs stiffen on Enoch's arms. An ancient fear is rising now, fills his lungs, clogs his breath.

Everything is exactly as it was. Maps and charts; meteorological computations; the cork noticeboard tacked with layers of notes; the crystal sets, the Hertz transmitters, the soldering iron, the Morse set and the CB radio, the magnetic tape reels and the miniature printing press. And before him, Frank's listening device. Enoch pulls away the sheet.

The machine is covered in cobwebs. Sprouting from a central patch bay, bales of wire and aerials twist into double helixes and figure-eights, metal wool brambles run amok. Headphones hang on the handle of a vice, bleeding static. Enoch sets down the gun and slips them on. Through the haze he can hear faint bleeps, long ones and short ones: *dit-dah-dit*, but he cannot comprehend the message it transmits.

Here now is Enoch's tragedy. He has never known the mind of Frank the shadow-man, Frank the absent husband, absent human being, Frank the genius, Frank the bogeyman, Frank the whizz, Frank the madman, Frank the visionary, Frank the boy with the crystal radio sets, Frank the immigrant mick, Frank the soldier who learned the hard way that a man must kill or be butchered like cattle on the killing ground. He has never known the mind of the Frank who endured the wastelands of Korea in temperatures that sank to minus forty, where the ground was so hard you couldn't dig in, not even with a pick, where you had to bury your feet in sand-bags to keep your toes from freezing off. The mind of Sergeant Frank O'Reilly who received an honour-able discharge then returned home and married and sired and spent his life in service of an obsession while his wife and child went wanting for a man and not a shadow of a man. Frank who scowled at the sound of Elvis, Frank the mad inventor, Frank the water dowser, Frank the disappeared, Frank the sudden death, Frank the maybe-suicide, Frank the phantom, Frank the revenant, the ghost.

Enoch peers at the machine's monitor. In the top right-hand corner, the date and time, his father's name, and a readout –

+ + THERE ARE 0 DAYS TO THE FLOOD + +

– and now the screen flurries with numbers, dot-matrix clusters that come apart and reconfigure as an image begins to form. Enoch puts his hand against the glass to block the glare and the screen sizzles against his skin, and when he looks again it's as if he's been given new eyes to comprehend the image frozen behind the screen, submerged in sine-wave crests and troughs that might be representations of brain activity patterns or the currents of a river, for there he sees his father's face, Frank O'Reilly's face, and now the devils begin to hiss and the sound in Enoch's ears is deafening, the whirling chopper blades, the *whomp* of herons' wings, the coming of the rain, the roaring of the flood, rivers babbling on and on, everything, everything but the sound of the Holy Ghost Radio.

No preacher's voice. No revelation. No *I know this*.

Enoch knows nothing, and this nothingness persists until he can stand it no more and grips the shotgun stock between his knees. He stares into the two dark eyes of its twin barrels and observes the true colour of oblivion.

+ + + + + + + +

The Holy Ghost Radio Is on the Air

31 October 1984

+ + + + tango hotel echo + + + +

+ + + + romeo india victor echo romeo + + + +

+ + + + india sierra + + + +

+ + + + charlie oscar mike india november golf + + + +

+ + + + india november tango oscar + + + +

+ + + + hotel echo romeo + + + +

+ + + + tango india mike echo + + + +

Transmission begins at 24.00 hours, 31 October 1984. Signal of unknown origin. At first it manifests as sheets of static, the *schhh* of a detuned television, and then through the white noise's wall of fire, faint at first but growing stronger, a succession of short sharp dashes and dots that infiltrate every frequency in Murn.

Listen and you will hear it blare from taxis' and squad cars' radios, from the loudspeakers at the dog track, the intercom in St Edmund's, the wooden-panelled amplifiers mounted above the cenotaph in

St Cecilia's cathedral, the stereo systems and Peavey amplifiers in Brown's Electrical, the banks of IBMs in the Vocational School's computer room, the franking machine in the County Council offices, the Bose bass bins in the Rua Hotel's ballroom.

It transmits through Owen Cody's Sony Walkman and Alice Stafford's now disused office line and the Citizen's Band radio in Isaac Miller's van and Iggy Ellis's walkie-talkie and Nicky Wickham's ghetto blaster and the antique radio under lock and key in Professor Stafford's dusty abandoned office and the jukebox into which Billy Litt pumps coins in the Island Inn, but none of them attempt decipherment. And outwards it spreads and its warning dissipates as a dreamer's memory of the dream, yet further outwards it spreads, each blip like a pebble skimmed across the airwaves and beyond.

Can you hear it, brothers and sisters?

The Holy Ghost Radio is on the air.

+ + + + + + + +

Andy Caffrey Pulls the
Graveyard Shift

1 November 1984, 12.01 a.m.

Midnight Mike rings in sick and someone needs to cover Ballo Local's graveyard shift. Andy Caffrey takes the call, which means last-minute cancellation of girlfriend-related plans and next thing the old lady is bending his ear with Andy this and Andy that and Andy it's not like this is even a proper paying gig, and Andy thinks it's not work hon, it's a calling.

Which is how he ends up sequestered in the Marconi Suite in the dead of night with only a Ziploc of Mary-Jane resin and a stack of LPs for company. He's just zoning out to Zeppelin's 'Battle of Evermore' when the vibe is obliterated by the most obnoxious noise.

Andy sits up in his swivel chair and parks his spliff in an ashtray and pushes the master fader up to better hear these abstract dots and dashes bleeding through the blasts of static. He can't decide if he should ring Malachy this late or ignore the problem until it goes away.

But it does not go away. Finally Andy decides there's nothing for it but to contact the boffins at Ballo Lighthouse. The nightwatch down the Horn confirms their signal has indeed been compromised, not just theirs but everybody's – but worry not, for HQ in Dublin's got a trace on the rogue transmission's origin, which appears to be somewhere around Ballo Manor, the big old house beyond Mweelrooney. The old O'Reilly residence, Andy realises.

He opens the window to clear the studio of fumes then locates the keys to his Volkswagen Beetle and locks up the Marconi Suite and gets on the road. As the lights of Murn shrink in his rearview mirror he flips the radio on and twists the dial and all stations are broadcasting the same signal through the static, even the national broadcaster, and he shakes his head in wonderment as another sequence of blips resounds across the airwaves like some esoteric Angelus.

He manages to roll a one-skinner as he drives and smokes it almost to the roach. The old coast route goes right through Ballo Harbour, penetrating deep into the Horn, zigging and zagging between tall stone walls that hold the barren fields at bay. The signal grows clearer, louder, and Andy tracks it, speeding past the seal-sheltering coves where waves riot against rocks sent here by glacial drift two million years ago, past slabs of mudstone and siltstone and sandstone, pebbles and cobbles and shale, shell fossils and cockles and coral and quartz. Ballo Lighthouse looms like some construction from a fairy tale, the oldest of its kind, once run by friars and fuelled on whale oil, now seriously state of the art.

Onwards towards the peninsula's tip, and the signal's growing louder yet. There on flat, unlandscaped land, stands Ballo Manor. Andy steers the little Beetle up a narrow, stony lane, slowing the car to spare the shocks and suspension, all the while cooing words of encouragement.

The front door of Enoch's pad is open. A crow banger or a gun's report shatters the stillness of the night. It takes a moment to register that the signal on the radio has stopped and there's only dead air now, total radio silence. Andy commits himself to action and forces his skinny frame from behind the wheel. He crosses the yard and pauses at the open door and it takes all the gumption he's got to cross the threshold and call out Enoch's name. Inside there's nothing only darkness and a fungal smell and the acrid residue of something burnt. By the flame of his Zippo he sees an open cellar trapdoor right under his hiking boots. Crouched at the lip of the abyss, he gazes down.

'Horse?' he says. 'You there?'

The Zippo is getting hot. He switches it to his other hand and descends the steps to the cellar. Bits of glass crunch underfoot. The lighter's flame trembles as he squints about. By the flickering light he sees it: a heap of smoking, twisted metal atop a splintered workbench. Chunks of blackened circuitry are flung all over the floor. Busted headphones and cut ringlets of wire, a shattered teacup and a tipped bottle of Glenfiddich. Spent shotgun shells everywhere. Beneath the bench, a tongue of teletype paper protrudes from some sort of printing press.

Andy stoops as if assisting a birth, and takes the paper in his hand and reads by the light of the flame.

To whom it may concern,

Like the druid Finegas I have fished for the Salmon of Knowledge, not in the streams of the earth, but in those of the air.

In the event that I do not return from the river, I bequeath my research materials, equipment and the patents of all inventions to my son Enoch. Now I must go down to the Rua to conclude my work. Tonight I go diving for the salmon.

Frank O'Reilly

Andy scrolls down the teletype. He's about to tear it

off and stuff it in his combat jacket when the printing press clanks into life and begins chattering and spewing more rolls of paper. The teletype unfurls itself into Andy's hands, reams of the stuff.

By the light of the wavering flame, Andy begins to read.

+ +

ovember 1 1.04am 1984
  608FOR44 32234

BULLETIN – IMMEDIATE BROADCAST
REQUESTED

  FLOOD WARNING

CC NATIONAL METEOROLOGICAL SERVICE, BALLO
LIGHTHOUSE, BALLO LOCAL RADIO, THE BALLO
VALLEY SENTINEL, MURN COUNTY COUNCIL

  ETF 1233 PM 1984

SGT F O'REILLY HAS ISSUED A FLOOD WARNING
FOR THE FOLLOWING: RIVER RUA AND BALLO
HARBOUR AFFECTING MURN AND ENVIRONS

HEAVY RAINFALL THURSDAY NOON NOV 1 WILL

CAUSE RIVER TO RISE RAPIDLY. MAJOR
FLOODING IS FORECAST . . . THE RIVER WILL
RISE ABOVE FLOOD STAGE AROUND 7 AM
MONDAY AND CREST NEAR 18.0 FEET AROUND
5 AM WEDNESDAY. THE RIVER WILL FALL
BELOW FLOOD STAGE FOLLOWING THURSDAY
AFTERNOON.

PRECAUTIONARY/PREPAREDNESS ACTIONS TO
FOLLOW:

+ +

every thing that is in the earth shall die STOP I know this

+ +

for it is Noe who is the second Adam to whom the men of all
the world are traced STOP For the Flood drowned the whole
seed of Adam STOP Afterwards when God brought a Flood
over the whole world none of the people of the world es-
caped from the Flood except it be the people of that ark
STOP Ut dixit poeta

+ +

E RIVER KNOWS WHAT TIME IT IS.

+ +

and the waters shall no more become a flood to destroy all

+ +

MONTH OF NEVEREMBER/WHE

+ +

why

+ +

HE RIVER IS COMING INTO HER TIME THE
RIVER IS COMING INTO HER TIME THE RIVER IS
COMING INTO HER TIME THE RIVER IS COMING
INTO HER TIME THE RIVER IS COMING INTO
HER TIME THE RIVER IS COMING INTO HER
TIME

+ +

+ + + + + + + +

IX

NEVEREMBER

+ + + + + + + +

The Flood

The first drop falls from the frowning heavens and strikes the ground at noon. Drum taps, scattershot at first, then the rhythms intensify and here it comes, a thousand drummers in syncopation, ratamacues, paradiddles and flams, until certain of those rhythms break formation and the patterns fall apart and liquefy and then reconstitute in freeform, a vindictive drizzle that beats the surface of the streets until they shine and the gutters gurgle with dirty sluicewater and sodden leaves litter the roads and clog the drains.

Three days it perseveres, and even the gabbing jackdaws hush beneath its onslaught. The river's current quickens and swells around the bridge's supporting struts and now the Rua shows its true colour, a murky, dirty red. First the sandbars go under, then the slipways, then the torrent gains the banks' rims, threshing and frothing through the concourse like a beast, and those old enough to remember other floods know it's only a matter of hours and hush their young to catch the forecast on the wireless. Folk reinforce doorways with sandbags and floodgates and shift all valuables upstairs. The hotel's guests gather in the observatory tower, a rapture cult gazing heavenward, and a lake of rain falls upon Murn in a single weekend.

The Rua breaches its banks. Within hours the town's maps are redrawn, the promenade and the river roads submerged, fields are turned to swamp, cattle marooned on meadows that are new-made islands. For a week the town is besieged by flood. Landslides slump into the current, thickening the river's broth, and as a muddy tide mounts the slope and moves towards the railway tracks the halls of the psychiatric hospital resound with patients' cries and howls. Now the pens in the town's abattoir succumb to the torrent and the poor pigs are swept. Panicked, squealing beasts open their throats with their trotters as they try to paddle through the mire.

At last the downfall slackens and slowly the waters withdraw, and for a while it seems the worst is past. Then, by the eighth day of the month, local radio is crackling with word of the first drowning. The shock of it is like a declaration of martial law or national emergency. Rescue teams meet by the boat-house at first light, faces grim and businesslike as they pull wet gear from their cars and sip from flasks or snatch a last smoke before readying themselves to enter the world beneath this world, a realm of weeds and fronds and murk, and God knows what they'll find before this day is out. Each man's face is tight as he falls backwards from his dinghy and breaks the water with a splash.

Community wardens line the bank, monk-like in oilskins and wellingtons, scanning the current with binoculars, ready to drop an orange buoy or to radio headquarters on sight of a floater. They keep death-watch around the clock, these sentinels, fluorescent jackets lurid in the mist.

Bodies are reclaimed – the first burials begin. Long black cars crawl from church to road to grave-yard. In their wake men lean on their women, women on their men, arms linked and all eyes down-ward cast. Bettors hunch on stoops and drinkers in pub doorways glare at each passing hearse with what looks almost like hatred or contempt. Gallows jokes circulate and rumours of copycat incidents leap from one tongue to the next, rumours of men opening their veins before walking in, rumours of drowners refusing life-rings.

Waves of shock proceed outwards to the furthest extremities of the town. By the third week the toll is up to eight and the tragedies have taken on the air of some dark festival. Local newspaper headlines blare in seventy-two-point type, though the word suicide is never used. Reports simply say that a man was seen entering the river at such and such a point at such and such a time, and those who write them are torn between duty to the unmediated truth and the bounds of professional ethics. Intruders at a public funeral, they exist on the other side of what is happening, bound to witness but not to intervene. Murn must face this trial on its own.

Now the parish priest Father John Callaghan ascends to the pulpit of St Cecilia's to voice his plea of why, raising his face as though tracing the echo generated by that word as it flutters about the church, a single syllable that divides itself into many, echoes giving unto echoes that proliferate into a symphony of tiny sounds that appears to the priest almost visible. And there is no answer, only multiple signals inhabiting a single channel, the many whys that fragment and multiply, the question squared, the question cubed, the question made exponential.

He calls what has transpired here a silent holocaust, a phrase that is later quoted in the local papers and on radio. But no man's words will sway the river. The Rua goes on taking until at last, obeying some unknowable intelligence, she takes no more.

And now Murn is consumed by a silence and stillness as terrible as the flood's roar. The town is stricken with it, you can feel the weight of it in the air, the pressure of what can't be said, as though certain thoughts must not be articulated openly but hissed, like an oath or curse. As though to explicitly acknowledge the thought might transmit it. The why is never answered, for this dark festival has ended, the sideshows are taken down, the macabre carnival moved on. There is by unspoken consent a sort of mass forgetting, a communal blotting out.

And yet in their haunted hours certain townsfolk wonder if the drowned could have returned to the living in their dreams, beckoned their brothers to follow, and all succumbed to the curse they bore in common. A brotherhood of the flood, returned to the waters that spawned them, rebaptised not into the light but the darkness that existed before humankind. These townsfolk shiver at the notion of the river singing her culling song, her vapours infecting the thoughts of men, passing the kill-yourself command down and down the chain. Why: still the question seeks its answer, and only the few allow themselves to recall the floods and drownings of twenty-eight years before.

So sleep now brothers, say these townsfolk as the winter nights draw down. Sleep among the ghosts of your brothers before you. Sleep among the minnows and the fronds. May your souls sleep upon the river bed, and never wake, for your suffering is done. Sleep now brothers, until the end of time has come to Murn.

+ + + + + + + +

Epitaph

December 1984

The river is quiet tonight. Maybe she dreams of her ancient sisters, the Bann and the Sinaan, the Lee and the Boyne, the Blackwater, the Barrow, the Nore and the Suir, the Lagan, the Liffey and the Foyle. Perhaps her shallows still harbour the fabled salmon that stole the sacred knowledge of the Tuatha Dé Danaan, those prideful spawn of the goddess Danu who ruled the seas and controlled the winds from their isle of the ever young.

Once, long ago, hooded river deities gathered here in summit to be anointed by Manannán, the lord of the sea, with his long green streels of hair and webbed fingers, sprawled upon his throne of jet-black coral. Once gods' faces moved across these waters and newborn stars silvered the shallows and the first inklings of the human race spawned there on her bed. Much later men raised a settlement by the river and christened it Murn because of a plague that strifed its founders, and they named the river the Rua because of its colour when in flood.

Only fragments of that time remain. A portal tomb upon a hill: backstone, sidestone, roof and sill. A cairn of earth and stone. Ring forts and fairy raths. Pottery, tools and implements, standing stones aligned with the rising sun. Earthen mounds, burial sites, cists and pits, cinerary urns, cremation places. Animal pelts and torcs and armlets and votive offerings.

Here men of old milled and farmed and dried their corn in kilns and learned to work with iron. They sired children who grew to be men who hunted and tilled this soil in turn, and the women bore their babies and laboured beside their men. Normans came and raised this place from a settlement to a town. Franciscans built their friary, Augustinians their priory, laymen their forges and tanneries and pits. And here it was said there lived a great bellicose beast who guarded a sacred island in the current's fork, a fearsome thing with bristles and mane and crimson eyes and nails of iron that struck sparks upon the rock, and its fiery breath and belly were like a bellows, and its great whale's tail made the river boil. Then a hallowed saint received a vision in which the archangel Raphael instructed him to banish this water-dragon. The saint invoked his Father, Son and Holy Ghost and said to the beast depart, and the beast did depart, and that is how the word of Christ was brought to Murn.

Time has turned its mill and churned the days. Gods have replaced the elements, druids replaced the gods, saints replaced the druids, priests replaced the saints, merchants replaced the priests. The river has seen it all. The Rua will always flow, obeying cycles immemorial. Water falls from the heavens upon the mountain, and the mountain begets the stream, which begets the river, which begets the sea, which under the sun evaporates and reconstitutes as cloud high in the heavens before it falls afresh and becomes the river once again. Always this never-ending river. She has always been and will always be, flowing out of the past that was once future, into future times to come.

But tonight her waters are quiet, lit by yellow lights affixed to the arching bridge. The slope of Blackberry Hill provides the backdrop, traveller clans' rubbish strewn across the barren hill all the way to the craggy peak. Now the cold wind holds its breath. The mists part, revealing a memorial stone upon the western bank, as yet untainted by wind and rain.

Frank O'Reilly (January 1925–September 1969, recovered
November 1984)
Owen Cody (March 1966–November 1984)
Nicholas Wickham (May 1966–November 1984)
Ignatius Ellis (August 1958–November 1984)
Alice Stafford (September 1957–November 1984)
William Litt (May 1958–November 1984)
Isaac Miller (November 1958–November 1984)
Charles Stafford (January 1928–November 1984)
Unknown (Recovered November 1984)

+ +

why

+ +

HE RIVER

+ +

DAYS TO THE FLOOD

+ +

When Enoch had talked to the people, the Lord sent darkness onto the earth, and there was darkness, and it covered those men standing and talking with Enoch, and they took Enoch up onto the highest heaven, where the Lord was, and he received him and placed him before his face, and darkness left the earth, and light came again.

The Book of the Secrets of Enoch

Epilogue: The Rambling Man

Fifty-Six Years After the Flood

When darkness falls and shadows creep, the towns-folk gather their young and whisper tales of an old homeless soul who roams the gloaming with his black frock coat flapping against his tight black strides, a supernatural class of man, maybe a manit-ou who can make himself into a raven or a snake, a child guzzler, a cradle snatcher, a man with scars on his shoulders where once were wings and on his tail-bone where once there hung a dung-stained tail. And maybe after dark certain errant children will dare each other to climb out windows and shimmy pipes and scurry down the prom and put their ears to the railway tracks to count his approaching steps, and then sprint away shrieking, in sport at first. Yes, there goes abroad this autumn night a rambling man.

His ragged brogues beat upon the highways and the moors and dales and meadows. He treads the time-hewn tracks that split the paddocks and circumnavigate the brooks and bestride the grassy pastures and the plains, and there is resonance in the sound of those heels and toes that strike the frost-hard ground like gavels. This ancient shadow-man tramps in the footprints of giants. Con of the Hundred Battles. Nuada of the Silver Hand. Creidne the artificer and Goibhnen the smith, Gann and Genann and Eochaid Mac Eirc. Mobius the flat-faced and Enda Dearg and the prophet Beg Mac De. Elim of the Great Wine Snow and Cairbre the Cat-headed. What names they had, these mongrel spawn of gods and men.

This man has long lost track of clocks and calendars. He marks time by sun's rising and moon's term, the turn of leaves and the flights of birds. His snow-white hair falls past his shoulders and a beard hangs from his jaw like heather from a crag. Flesh has melted from his bones, first the gut, then the face, then from his mighty haunches. He is in a metamorphic state, a state of rebecoming.

He remembers this state from when he was a young man many years ago, stout of heart, with a cast-iron neck and big brass balls, when he knew in his marrow what his mind did not. Since then he has endured scores of winters upon this earth. He was born on the tip of the Horn peninsula. He knew of fame and infamy, praise and ridicule the same. He knew glory and grief but hardly love, and in the end was summoned home to suffer figurative death and then resurrection.

An age of exile then. Some say for years he wandered the valleys of Wales, raving to any Christian who would listen. Some say they saw him stood upon a fruit crate in Covent Garden, demanding to know if passers-by had heard the true voice of the Holy Ghost Radio. Some said he served as a mercenary in the Congo or the Southern Sudan armed with an AK-47, proclaiming himself the Elvis Avenger. He spent many moons walking to and fro upon the earth, and up and down upon it, but now after more than half a century abroad in the world he has returned to his native soil, these woods around Mweelrooney.

He once was weary from his wandering, for far and wide he's strayed, but now as he roams the gloaming a revival of the soul is in effect, a sense of being birthed a second time. Great muscles are again in contraction, forcing him on towards his fate. Something awaits him out there in the woods.

+ + + + + + + +

Now, in Heavendale there is a public wood, the only part of the county spared the blades of the sawmill's hirelings and the roundheads' axes long before them. No country of stumps, this. Planted land, rich with imported species. Trees loom in the half-light like tribal elders: giant Lebanese cedars fleshed with soft moss, weeping beeches dripping green veils, oriental spruce, chestnut and fir so monstrous you'd fancy they contain casked chieftains of times long past.

And here is the biggest oak in Europe. Press your face against the rough bark and embrace the tree's girth and maybe you will feel the raw coursing of its resin blood and hear the beat of the earth's great heart transmitted from the soil. Beyond is a stand of poppies, their violet stamens like the petals of sea anemones. Then a copse, and then a clearing, in the centre of which sits a pile of branches on blackened scutch. There's a give in the ground. You might be treading on a mattress.

A hare skedaddles through the rushes into gathered sycamores, the hanging woods where tormented souls rope themselves to beams and jump, and you can picture their spirits' swinging shadows, midges drinking from eyes and tongues, and the stains under twitching toes where mandrake will sprout, fertilised by their seed. Aye, this place has *energy*.

The rambler cocks his head. Water churns nearby. Ahead in the gloom is a system of waterfalls and a hydro-electrical station. Across a bridge ridged with tree roots there looms the hulk of an old watermill. Rapids show their teeth. The rambler fills his lungs and roars as loud as he is able, but he can scarcely hear himself above the cascades' din.

Froth feeds into pools where the threshing becomes tranquil. Into a deep, forbidding wood the rambler goes. Concealed behind brush and brambles and briars is an overgrown wheelhouse or hunter's lodge. The rambler approaches and forces the door – it is dark inside. He strikes a match, finds an oil lamp, lights the wick and casts his eyes about the hut and sees words inscribed on the walls.

> *iver when the night draws down and all is still i*
> *hear your voice you speak in riverish now i know*
> *only riverality and so this night i take up my rod*
> *and listen to your song for the sound of the river*
> *river is the sound of thought itself like the babble*
> *of your waters the river the river the river the*
> *river*

Now the rambler scowls and casts about. Sunk into

the middle of the floor is a well-hole. Suspended over this, a winch. Rope plunges into the blackness. He peers into the well and gives the crank a half-hand's turn. Over the complaint of the rusty mechanism, a faint clatter can be heard.

He cranks the handle a dozen turns and the clattering grows louder and soon a metal pail emerges from the hole. He lifts it out. Inside is a hazel rod, perhaps a yard in length, culminating in a slender fork. His fingers tighten on the shaft and the bark appears to throb.

He quenches the lamp and leaves the cabin and returns to the night with the hazel wand. The wood feels good and strong and his body seems to reposition of its own accord, arms extended, fingers tight around the stem.

He's no more than a hundred yards gone before the hair stiffens on his arms and the rod comes alive and quivers and then dips. His pulse quickens as his wrists rotate, sensing what's in store, but no inkling nor intuition can diminish the shock of what happens next. The rod plummets violently down, almost wrenched clear from his grip. Sweat prickles between his shoulder blades and something shudders just below that and now he feels it right enough, raw voltage down the spine, into the perineum, right in the fucking root, a surge of blood the like of which he has not felt in thirty years or more.

Now comes the climax, announced by a grunt from the throat, the charge so unexpected he reels backwards, stumbles, trips, ends up on his haunches. There he sits, stunned and startled, all paroxysm and muscle spasm and aftershock. Then a memory of his father closing his fingers around an electric fence and simultaneously grabbing his wrist and the laughs of the old bastard as the jolt ran through them both.

It isn't until the tremors have subsided that the rambler registers the dampness on his leg. He unbuttons his tight black trousers and tugs at his undergarments and takes a look. He plucks up a dock leaf and wipes himself. Then he takes up his rod and walks.

It is thirteen days to the flood.

+ + + + + + + +

Now come feverish nights when it's unclear whether the bearer holds the hazel wand, or the hazel wand is an extension of the bearer's hands. By day he lays his aged body down in beds of leaves and drinks from streams and eats the fruit of the bushes, then come the fall of night he sets out with his rod, a new-sprouted limb that twitches and sniffs for water deposits or repositories set beneath the sediments of shell and stone, flint and coal, bone and mulch, peat and pan.

Across the blasted heath he roams, vectoring the territories, meadows heavy with heather, glades and glens speckled with bracken, sloblands and bogs and moors and fens, and all the while that forked prosthetic hums like an aerial attuned to the babbling of blind springs and geodetic spirals and sunken veins, all the buried songlines of the Rua's myriad tributaries.

Through wind and rain, through mist and fog, the rambling man roves out. Over bog and burn, through the Leper's Gap, the Devil's Elbow and the Fairy Faythe, diagramming the land with his wand. He beats through brambles and furze and inhales the melting chocolate scent of gorse and once, in a paddock wild with reeds, the rod wobbles and he gets a ripe, meaty smell and stumbles over a smear of mare's fresh placenta on the grass, already sunblackened and bubbled.

But this journeying is worth every step, for when the rod locates the water cell and throbs and thrums and causes its bearer to thrum and throb in turn, the downward yank is so violent and correct it near sucks him into the earth. The rush of blood brings forth a shudder, a suppuration. And in the aftermath he lies upon his back and gazes at the constellations, and it's worth it, yes, all the suffering a man endures upon the earth is worth it if it leads to this, for all the years have fallen from his flesh, sloughed off like so much dust.

But in a matter of hours the craving for another such spasm returns, and if he's to satisfy this lust he must seek the next source, because here's the thing: once a cell has been tapped it will not yield its pleasures again, and it is with foreboding and then full-blown dread that the rambling man realises that those pleasure cells distributed beneath the marl are dwindling.

There will be time for nothing else. Mark him now: the dope fiend seeks his dealer, the drunk his early house, and the rambler his bubble beneath the earth. He crawls from his sleeping place at dusk to roam the fields continually. When morning comes he sleeps until the sun goes down again, a handful of berries and a mouthful of water his only portion, and for weeks he neither glimpses nor speaks to another human soul.

His old life is a faded photograph, someone else's story, the names of those he once regarded as friends or enemies no more than minor personae in a half-forgotten play. Men knew him as Enoch O'Reilly, but it has been fifty-six years since he was last called by that name. Since then he has been a rambling man, an outcast under Heaven, exiled from his kind. A wretch of skin and bone who marches through the dark until the first rays of dawn warn him that soon the sun will crest over the hills and it will be time to take his rest again.

Some nights the moon confides its mysteries, hints at buried metals and gemstones, gold and oil, sacred gravesites and pockets of terrestrial radiation. It whispers of Pan and Theos, the all-is-god, and tells him nothing is unholy, that Nature and Un-nature are all the one. It tells him that men decry the freak and the abomination, but he too is part of God's design. For if the ruddy sun can best be apprehended by way of comparison with that pale and lunatic moon, if man can be nothing without woman, if graceful God is made whole by the baleful Devil, then surely the things that are of Nature have their equal but opposite reflection in the things of Unnature. The cast-out's purpose on this earth is to act as agent of this Unnatural, sent to define by contrast that which is commonly thought good and wholesome. For though ye be made to belly through the dirt, feared and despised by man, though ye have been decreed Unnatural, ye too are God's creation. So let them judge, for with what judgement ye judge, ye shall be judged, and with what measure ye mete, it shall be measured to you again.

Yes, the rambler hears all this intelligence, and sometimes stricken by his reflection in a pool, the image of the ancient wretch he has become, he swears blind he will quit this business of leys and lines, no more will the rambler go a-dowsing, for it has made of him a slave to an addiction, a mindless automaton, driven by the twitchings of his rod.

But his soul is too weak for the wean, and when he attempts to snap that wand across his knee he is beset by a burning gut and scrotum pain and a fever worse than that incurred by any want of junk or morphine. He sweats and soils himself but no matter how he scours his body with nettles in ice-cold streams none of it does a bit of good. By God he is rightly afflicted.

Worse, the cells keep on dwindling. It takes longer now to search them out, and he is lucky to locate one or two per night, and somewhere in the fissures of his brain a primal and unnamed instinct registers the tick and tock of a celestial clock as it counts down seven days to the next predicted flood, then six, then five, four, three, two, then one.

And so it comes to pass that by the last night of autumn all paths are finally walked, all deposits are tapped out. Forced inward from the wilds, the tired old rambler's paths contract in smaller orbits around the town of Murn and its silver river. Now comes the final reckoning.

The rambling man knows by the moon's cast that tonight is the feast of Samhain, when unseen forces are most potent, when the spirits of the dead are at their boldest and seek to penetrate the membrane that partitions us from them. As he creeps towards the town of Murn and the river that cleaves its heart he knows in his bones this is the last night he goes a-roving. The river knows it too, and the smoky wind, and the moon that shines all the brighter and has a blueish hue, and this evokes an air from another life, another time, blue moon, blue moon, how does it go again?

Now the hazel rod hums and a homing signal summons him towards the Rua river. There is a sense of unfolding, the certainty of what must happen. It was always bound to culminate in this: Enoch O'Reilly and the river, the river and Enoch O'Reilly, compelled towards their consummation.

The town of Murn is as quiet as a graveyard. The market square's deserted. The way is clear. He steps onto the bridge and mounts the wall over the central stanchion. He can hear the rushing current. The river is in heat. He grasps the thrumming wand, eyes shut tight, arms thrust out. The wood crackles static. Now dips the rod. Enoch's head snaps back, but there is no pleasure in this act.

The river screams, a piercing shriek that emits from the water's depths, no, deeper than that, the river beneath the river, where all rivers sing in unison of how it was in the beginning, in the barren and the soundless, the empty waste and the howling void, the devoid of everything, before a sound like a whale's call or swansong was heard as it sang itself into existence, a trickle at first, then a torrent that could not be contained by the banks of its own imagination, so it swelled and birthed itself out of eternity.

And still the river sings, sings of an ancient demiurge passing its great webbed hand over the face of the earth, quickening its pulse, wells exploding spumes like those of a leviathan, shooting columns of spray, geysering into the sky, flowering over the world, raising a flood, and the great sorrow that followed gave birth to human consciousness, for all knowing is all suffering and all thought is human pain.

And now the rambler joins his voice with hers, opens his throat and a sound comes forth that issues not from his own lungs but some otherworldly source using him as its horn.

'*You are listening to HOLY GHOST RADIO, transmitting for your benefit the sounds of the DEAD. Now hear this, heathen men. There were giants on the earth in ancient days. The sons of God came unto the daughters of men, and they bore children to them, and the same became mighty men which were of old, men of renown. And God saw that the wickedness of man was great in the earth, and that every thought of his heart was only evil continually. And it repented the LORD that He had made man on the earth, and it grieved Him at His heart.*'

And as the rambler roars these words he recalls their shapes from distant memory, declaims them to the wind, and as they are dispersed into the air he knows they will be snagged by the antennae of rusty old Sputniks or NASA hardware, bounced back through time to the year 1969, when these trigger words will be recognised by the aerials of his father's machine, snagged, sucked downward and then fed through the headphones clamped over the ears of the twelve-year-old boy he was, trespassing in his father's cellar – and that this is how young Enoch O'Reilly was possessed by the voice of the rambling man he would become. The sins of the father passed onto the son, the son become the father, the child the father of the man, father and son become rambling men, cursed upon the earth, fated to walk in footsteps preordained, through pathways of time recurring like loops, generations of possession, generations of floods, generations of forgetting, generations born again. At last Enoch O'Reilly has found the voice of the Holy Ghost Radio. It is his own.

'. . . And, behold, I, even I, do bring a flood of waters upon the earth, to destroy all flesh, wherein is the breath of life, from under heaven; and every thing that is in the earth shall die . . .'

His speech disintegrates into a language of no-language, and upon hearing this sound the river tells itself the time has come to flood again, flood again, summon the clouds, summon the rain, the heavy rains will come and she will guzzle them down and like a kraken she will rise and engulf the land.

For it is true, what was written and what was sung: there were giants on the earth in ancient times, men who believed they were gods, or gods who believed they were men. The Nephilim, the Archontes, the Fir Bolg, the Tuatha Dé Danaan, bold Oisín and Fionn MacCumhaill, and now Enoch O'Reilly takes his place among their number.

His eyes are opened. The wand in his hand is

wilted. He tosses it aside. The moon looms down, bathing the waters in silver light, and now counter to the current there sails a barge, gliding up the river. The barge draws near and closes on the bank. It is crewed not by mortal men but by three great birds with familiar ragged feathers and sideways-blinking eyes, who, before Enoch's own uncanny eyes, change their forms into the forms of crones.

Enoch descends to the water's edge. The heron-women take him in and lay him down and cover him with ermine. Now the boat returns downriver, and as Enoch O'Reilly observes the limitless sky, he feels a tiny sensation like a kiss upon his cheek.

The barge bears him away. He gazes at the heavens like a chieftain or a dying god made man returning to eternity.

Now comes the rain.

+ + + + + + + +